Michael Underwood and The Murder Room

>>> This title is part of The Murder Room, our series dedicated to making available out-of-print or hard-to-find titles by classic crime writers.

Crime fiction has always held up a mirror to society. The Victorians were fascinated by sensational murder and the emerging science of detection; now we are obsessed with the forensic detail of violent death. And no other genre has so captivated and enthralled readers.

Vast troves of classic crime writing have for a long time been unavailable to all but the most dedicated frequenters of second-hand bookshops. The advent of digital publishing means that we are now able to bring you the backlists of a huge range of titles by classic and contemporary crime writers, some of which have been out of print for decades.

From the genteel amateur private eyes of the Golden Age and the femmes fatales of pulp fiction, to the morally ambiguous hard-boiled detectives of mid twentieth-century America and their descendants who walk our twenty-first century streets, The Murder Room has it all. >>>

The Murder Room
Where Criminal Minds Meet

themurderroom.com

Michael Underwood (1916–1992)

Michael Underwood (the pseudonym of John Michael Evelyn) was born in Worthing, Sussex and educated at Christ Church College, Oxford. He was called to the Bar in 1939 and served in the British army during World War Two. He returned to work in the Department of Public Prosecutions until his retirement in 1976, and wrote almost 50 crime novels informed by his career in the law. His five series characters include Sergeant Nick Atwell and lawyer Rosa Epton, of whom is was said by the *Washington Post* that she 'outdoes Perry Mason'.

Rosa Epton
A Pinch of Snuff
Crime upon Crime
Double Jeopardy
Goddess of Death
A Party to Murder
Death in Camera
The Hidden Man
Death at Deepwood Grange
The Injudicious Judge
The Uninvited Corpse
Dual Enigma
A Compelling Case
A Dangerous Business
Rosa's Dilemma
The Seeds of Murder
Guilty Conscience

Goddess of Death

Michael Underwood

An Orion book

Copyright © Isobel Mackenzie 1982

The right of Michael Underwood to be identified as the author of this
work has been asserted in accordance with the Copyright, Designs and
Patents Act 1988.

This edition published by
The Orion Publishing Group Ltd
Orion House
5 Upper St Martin's Lane
London WC2H 9EA

An Hachette UK company
A CIP catalogue record for this book is available from the British Library

ISBN 978 1 4719 0463 9

www.orionbooks.co.uk

CHAPTER 1

'Gotcha!'

It may not have been the recognised formula for making an arrest, but it was effective, especially when uttered without warning and accompanied by a hug of which any bear could have been proud.

The victim gave one futile wriggle before his arm was twisted fiercely behind his back, abruptly cutting off any thought of escape.

'Gotcha!' P.C. Paynter said again, in a satisfied tone. He was a strapping young man who never needed a second invitation to demonstrate his physical prowess. Indeed, if truth be known, he felt cheated if deprived of an excuse for doing so when arresting somebody he regarded as fair game.

While this was going on, his colleague, P.C. Hexham, was faring less well. The second youth had given him a painful jab in the stomach with his elbow and taken to his heels almost before Hexham knew what was happening. With a good ten seconds start and a greater turn of speed than his pursuer, he was never in any danger of being caught.

P.C. Hexham returned out of breath and frustrated to where P.C. Paynter was standing with his prisoner in the shadow of a car.

'Got away, did he?' Paynter asked in a tone which barely concealed his contempt.

"Fraid so. He had too much of a start on me.'

'Search this one while I hold him,' Paynter ordered. He was the senior of the two by six months and liked to show who was in charge.

P.C. Hexham removed a wallet from a hip pocket of the arrested youth's jeans and some loose change from another pocket which he placed on the roof of the car beside which they were standing. A quick examination of the wallet revealed a driving licence, a snapshot of a girl in a bikini and £8 in notes.

'Take his keys,' Paynter said, nodding at a bunch which hung from a metal ring on the youth's belt.

'That seems to be the lot,' Hexham remarked in a faintly worried tone.

'It is,' the youth said angrily, speaking for the first time. 'So now you can let me go.'

'The only place you're going, boyo, is the station,' Paynter retorted, giving the arm he was holding a further twist for good measure. 'What's your name?'

'It's on my driving licence,' the youth said with a note of truculence, at the same time grimacing with pain.

'I'm asking you. What's your name?'

'You're breaking my arm.'

'Your name?'

'Arne. Francis Arne.'

'That's the name on the licence,' Hexham broke in quickly, as if hoping to defuse an embarrassing situation.

'Where do you live?'

'I haven't an address of my own.'

'Where'd you spend last night?'

'At a friend's flat in Hammersmith.'

'And the night before?'

'I've been there two or three weeks.'

'What's the name of your pal who buggered off?'

'I don't know his name. Anyway he's not a pal.'

'No? So what were you up to together?'

'We weren't up to anything. I'd never seen him before in my life.'

'You'd better think up something better than that.'

'It's the truth. What's more, if you don't let me go, I'll sue you for false arrest and assault.'

2

'You've a nerve! I don't take that sort of talk from little runts like you.'

'Let's get him back to the station,' Hexham broke in anxiously. Not for the first time in his short career, he cursed having been paired with Terry Paynter. The job was fraught with enough without having to go along with his rough-shod tactics.

On the way to their car which was parked round a corner, P.C. Paynter gazed thoughtfully at the bunch of keys taken from their prisoner and which he now held in his hand.

'I reckon some of these would open a few car doors,' he observed in a ruminative tone.

CHAPTER 2

Rosa Epton had just poured herself a second cup of tea when the telephone rang. At that hour in the morning (she had been up only half an hour) it usually meant her partner, Robin Snaith, on the line.

They were the sole partners of Snaith and Epton and were careful to keep one another in touch with their daily movements, if necessary leaving messages with Stephanie who was the office Girl Friday.

Rosa lifted the receiver on the kitchen extension.

'Is that Rosa Epton?' a voice asked urgently before she had time to speak. Though not Robin's, it was vaguely familiar.

'Yes.'

'This is Philip Arne. We've met once or twice and you came to a party when I moved into my flat.'

He was speaking in a gabble and Rosa broke in. 'Of course I remember you *and* the party.'

And, indeed, she did. She had first met Philip Arne in court. He was some sort of social worker and had had a professional interest in one of her clients, a Pakistani as she now recalled, charged with possession of marijuana. They had got on rather well and he had invited her to a party at his flat off Clapham Common, of which her chief memory was a sea of Asian faces and some extremely hotly-spiced snacks which had brought tears to the eyes.

'Oh that's a relief, because I certainly remember you very well,' he exclaimed. With a quick nervous laugh he went on, 'I apologise for calling you so early and at home but it's about my brother who's got into trouble. He's been arrested and is coming up in court this morning. Can you possibly go

4

along and represent him? I'd be tremendously grateful if you could.'

'What's he been charged with?'

'Under the hoary old sus law. They say he was tampering with parked cars, which is crazy for a start. Incidentally, I thought that law had been finally repealed.'

'It's about to be, but it'll be replaced by something not dissimilar. Which court is he appearing in?'

'Shepherd's Bush Magistrates' Court. That's not too far from where you live, is it?' he added hopefully.

'Not very.'

'I remember your telling me you had a flat in Campden Hill.'

'I still live there.'

'So can you go along..?' There was a distinct note of desperation in his voice.

'All right. I don't suppose the case'll be disposed of today. Indeed, if your brother's denying the charge, I'll have to ask for a remand.'

'He denies it completely. He was very agitated when he phoned me and said the whole thing was a frame-up. He'd been hauled off to the police station and despite his protests not been allowed to get in touch with me for several hours. But you're probably familiar with that scenario ...'

Rosa was, but refrained from comment. Instead she said, 'How old is your brother?'

'Nineteen. Twenty next month. There's eight years between us. By the way, his name is Francis.'

'Where does he live?'

'At the moment he's in a flat at Hammersmith. There are several others living there and a good deal of coming and going. You know what the young are like.'

'Does he have a job?'

'He's been drifting from one casual employment to the next. Like so many kids of his age, he's found it hard to settle down since leaving school.' He paused. 'But don't think the worse of him for that, Rosa! I'm very fond of him.'

'Will you be coming to court yourself, Philip?' she asked.

'Should I? I've got a fairly busy morning ahead of me.'

'If he's granted bail, which is a reasonable certainty, the police may ask for a surety. I imagine you'd be willing to stand?'

'Of course. I'd better try and re-arrange a couple of my appointments. Will it matter if I don't turn up till the end of the morning?'

'No, though he mayn't be released until you do appear.'

With a slight catch in his voice, he said, 'I can't tell you how grateful I am, Rosa. I was sure I could rely on you. I've always been the big brother to Francis and he's always turned to me when he's been in trouble.'

Did this mean previous trouble with the police, Rosa wondered? But that was something she'd find out soon enough.

'If I don't see you in court,' he went on, 'I'll call you at home this evening. I'll be anxious to hear what you think of the case and how you rate his chances.'

Though she had not seen Philip Arne for about three or four months, his face had been clearly in her mind's eye while they talked. He was near enough her own age and she had found him attractive, but after his party their professional paths had not crossed again and her half-expectation that he might invite her out had not been fulfilled. If he had done so, she would readily have accepted. On the other hand she hadn't brooded unduly over his failure to further their social relationship.

Shepherd's Bush Magistrates' Court was one in which she appeared regularly and where she had particular ties with its officials.

'Wasn't expecting to see you here this morning, Miss Epton,' the jailer greeted her.

'Up to a couple of hours ago, I wasn't expecting to be here,' Rosa replied with a smile. 'I believe you have someone called Francis Arne locked away in your dungeon.'

'Dungeon, indeed! We have the best cell accommodation in the whole of the M.P.D. We have old lags trying to make winter bookings because they find it so cosy here.' He glanced down at the list of overnight charges which was clipped to a millboard in his hand. 'P.C. Paynter's the officer. I suppose you'll be asking for a remand?'

'I've yet to take my client's instructions, but I don't imagine he'll want to plead guilty.'

'You could try and persuade him . . .'

Rosa grinned. 'It must be wonderful having such an optimistic nature. Incidentally, who's sitting today?'

'Mr Lipstead. You're his favourite amongst favourites. He drools every time you walk into court.'

'What nonsense!' Rosa said with an embarrassed laugh. She was not, however, unaware of the magistrate's tendency to bend over backwards to meet her wishes. It was a situation she had found embarrassing on a number of occasions. His readiness to accede to her every application placed an unfair burden on her not to take advantage of his pliancy.

'I suppose you want to see your client?' the jailer said genially

'Please.'

'Know him?'

'No.'

'I wish you luck with him.' Rosa raised a quizzical eyebrow and the jailer added, 'Arrogant-looking little so and so.'

Which was near enough Rosa's own impression when she was shown into his cell. He glanced up from the bench on which he was sitting, but apparently decided not to stir himself.

'My name's Rosa Epton. I'm a solicitor and a friend of your brother. He phoned me this morning and asked me to represent you.'

7

'Oh,' he said uncertainly, as he lifted his backside a token few inches off the bench in what Rosa took to be a gesture of acknowledgement. 'Did Philip tell you I'd been framed? It's crazy to suggest I was trying car doors.' In a tone of considerable bitterness, he added, 'They were obviously out to grab anyone they saw merely to bolster their statistics.'

'What were you actually doing when they arrested you?' Rosa asked.

'I was just taking a look at this old car. It was a vintage Rolls and I crossed the road to have a closer look at it.'

'Where was this?'

'In Kenpark Square.'

'Did you examine the other cars?'

'Definitely not.'

'Sure about that?'

'Of course I'm sure.'

'Could the police have thought you were going from car to car?'

'No way.'

'Did you touch the Rolls? Try its doors or anything like that?'

'No. The only time I touched it was when that bastard Paynter shoved me against it. He almost broke my arm. I want him charged with assault.'

'Were you examined by a doctor at the police station?'

He shook his head moodily. 'They wouldn't let me get in touch with anyone. They just tried to bully me into saying I'd plead guilty.'

'Who's they?'

'Mostly Paynter. There was a sergeant around for part of the time and there was this other constable who was with Paynter, but he wasn't too bad. If you ask me, he was embarrassed by Paynter's bullying behaviour.'

'What was the other officer's name?'

8

'I think it was Hexham. Something like that, anyway.'

Rosa nodded slowly. 'I think that's about all I need to know for the moment. It's obvious the case won't proceed today, so it's a question of getting you bail which shouldn't be difficult. Later you can come along to my office and I'll take a detailed proof of your evidence.'

He gave her a morose look. 'I'm afraid I haven't got any money.'

'I'll apply for legal aid.'

'Good, it's time I got something out of the taxpayer.' The observation was accompanied by a sour little smile which Rosa had pointedly ignored.

It was clear to her that in the distribution of charm between the two brothers, Philip had scooped the jackpot. Francis had the air of a spoilt, dissatisfied child. He was of slight physique, had naturally curly hair and a mouth that turned down at the corners. His eyes gave him a permanently hostile expression. And yet overall he was a good-looking boy, even unshaven after a night in a police cell.

He has the slightly depraved air of a fallen cherub, Rosa decided as she covertly studied him.

As she returned through the jailer's office on her way to court, a burly young P.C. stepped from a throng of waiting officers.

'I'm P.C. Paynter,' he said in a faintly truculent tone. 'I believe you're defending Arne?'

'That's right. I'll be asking for a remand, if that's what you want to know.'

'I reckon you'll advise him to plead guilty when you know all the facts.'

'At the moment I know very few of the facts and it's definitely a plea of not guilty,' Rosa retorted with a touch of acerbity.

'I suppose he thinks because his pal escaped, he'll be able

9

to wriggle out of it,' Paynter remarked with something between a smile and a sneer.

Rosa managed to conceal her surprise, something lawyers become adept at doing. Francis Arne had certainly made no mention of being with someone else. His omission served to confirm her fear that defending Philip's brother was going to be neither an easy nor, probably, a very satisfactory experience.

Mr Lipstead was already on the bench when she entered court. He was a tubby, avuncular man of normally benign manner, who was nevertheless capable of flying into sudden rages, when his face would redden and his dewlaps quiver with menace. These outbursts would pass with the suddenness of a tropical storm and were induced, more often than not, by a witness or a lawyer whose face or behaviour he unaccountably took against. Caught without warning or protection in the epicentre of the storm, the victim could only wait for it to abate, which it did with a final angry rumble.

As soon as he saw Rosa come in, he gave her a welcoming smile which she returned with a small bow. Having dispatched the item of business that had been occupying him, he turned to give her his full attention.

'In what way can the court help you, Miss Epton?' he enquired in his friendliest tone.

'I represent Francis Arne, sir, who is number eight on your list of charges. It's a plea of not guilty and I shall be asking for a remand.'

'So you'd like the case called immediately, I expect, and then you can get away?'

'I'd greatly appreciate that, sir, if it doesn't inconvenience the court.'

'We're here to assist, Miss Epton. No point in your hanging around if the case is for remand.'

Mr Lipstead glanced toward the jailer who had had the

prescience to position Francis at the head of the queue of defendants lined up in the corridor outside.

'Charge number eight, Francis Arne,' he intoned as he opened the door and gave the defendant a brisk beckoning nod.

'I take it there's no objection to bail?' the magistrate said, addressing himself to P.C. Paynter who was hovering close to the witness box.

Paynter took a step forward and assumed a bullish look.

'The defendant has no fixed abode, your worship,' he said bluntly.

Mr Lipstead's expression clouded over slightly. 'Are you saying that you do oppose bail?'

'The defendant can offer a surety, sir,' Rosa broke in quickly.

'Are you still opposing bail in the light of what Miss Epton has just said?'

It was not the first time P.C. Paynter had incurred Mr Lipstead's disfavour, though his skin was too thick ever to show any scars.

'No, your worship, but I think the surety should be substantial.'

'That's a matter for the court,' Mr Lipstead remarked in his judicially reproving tone. Addressing Francis he went on, 'You'll be remanded on bail in your own recognisance of £25 and with one surety in the sum of £250.' Turning to Rosa and leaning forward in his chair as if about to offer her a plate of sandwiches, he said, 'How long a remand would you like, Miss Epton?'

The jailer glanced across at the court inspector and raised his eyebrows skywards. It's a wonder he doesn't have us serving her clients with hot drinks and tasty snacks, he reflected sardonically.

'My client doesn't wish to have the charge hanging over his head for longer than necessary, sir, but I know how full your list is with fixtures.'

'Your first free morning for a contested case is June the twenty-sixth,' the jailer said defiantly.

'We must try and fit it in before then,' Mr Lipstead said in an equally firm tone. 'Three and a half months is too long to keep a young man waiting on such a charge.' The jailer fixed his unblinking gaze on the coat of arms on the wall behind the magistrate's chair and remained silent. 'I'll remand him for two weeks,' Mr Lipstead went on. 'We're used to juggling with the list,' he added, carefully avoiding looking in the jailer's direction.

Rosa collected up her papers and, giving the magistrate a courteous bow, edged her way out of court. She had met Maurice Lipstead socially on a number of occasions when he was usually under the restraining influence of a particularly watchful wife. His third, so Rosa understood. Despite her presence he had, nevertheless, contrived to give Rosa a smacking kiss beneath the mistletoe at a court Christmas party on one occasion. It was rumoured that his wife had since put him on a shorter lead when they went out together.

Outside the court Rosa passed behind P.C. Paynter, who was talking to another officer.

'We've got to find his mate,' Paynter said vehemently. 'He obviously got away with all the stuff.'

His colleague's only response was a forlorn nod.

Rosa had little doubt about whom they were talking. But what stuff, she wondered as she moved out of earshot?

CHAPTER 3

Thanks to Mr Lipstead, Rosa was back at her office soon
after eleven o'clock. She was due in another court at two to
mitigate on behalf of a motorist who, according to police
evidence, had ricocheted across Hammersmith Broadway at
3 a.m. leaving a trail of destruction that included three
damaged parked cars, two shattered bollards and a lamp post
in which he met his final match. She had warned him that he
was bound to lose his licence and be heavily fined, if not be
sent to prison. Fortunately, nobody had been hurt in the
course of the car's wild escapade and her client was
a first offender, both of which gave Rosa some scope for
mitigation.

She had been at her desk for just over an hour when
Stephanie informed her on the internal phone that a Mr
Arne had walked into reception and asked to see her.

'Which Mr Arne?' Rosa enquired with a slight frown.

'Hold on and I'll find out,' said the unflappable Stephanie,
to supply the answer a few seconds later. 'Mr Francis Arne.'

Rosa glanced at her watch. She supposed she could see
him now, though it irked her that he had just turned up
expecting to walk in without any semblance of an appointment. Philip had obviously been to court and signed as a
surety and Francis must have come straight from there to his
solicitor's office. Perhaps at Philip's suggestion, or, more
likely, because he couldn't think of anything better to do
with his time. In any event the sooner she saw him, the
sooner she'd find out.

'All right, Stephanie, send him in,' she said, reaching for a
large pad of paper and then pushing back her hair which had
fallen forward on either side of her face. It was a habit, if the

13

truth be known, that always gave Mr Lipstead a distinctly sensual pleasure.

A minute later the door opened and Francis came in.

He gave her a small nod. 'Philip told me I should come and see you straight away, so I have.'

'You're lucky to find me free. Next time make an appointment or you may have a wasted journey.'

He appeared unmoved by the reproof and stood glancing about her office with mild interest.

'Pretty functional, isn't it?'

'What were you expecting, thick pile carpeting and furnishings from Heals?'

'From what Philip told me, I thought there'd be a few feminine touches amongst the dusty tomes.'

'And what exactly *did* Philip tell you?' Rosa asked, and immediately regretted it.

'That you were the most feminine of all the female lawyers he'd come across. He also said you were pretty good.' As he spoke he fixed her with a cool, appraising stare.

Rosa was silent for a moment, then said briskly, 'Now we'd better discuss more important things, namely your case.' She picked up her pen and poised it purposefully over the pad of paper. 'For a start, I gather from the police you were with someone else who ran away. Is that right?'

He stared down at the floor for a few seconds before replying in an almost offhand tone, 'No, I was on my own.'

Rosa frowned. 'Are the police mistaken then?'

'There was this other chap who was also looking at the car, but we weren't together. We just happened to be there at the same moment.'

'Was it dark?'

'Yes.'

'Wasn't it rather a curious time to be examining the finer points of a vintage Rolls?'

He gave a shrug. 'Not to me.'

'Was there a street lamp nearby?'

14

'No idea. There was enough light from somewhere.'

'And you crossed the road to where this car was parked.'

'That's right.'

'As I recall Kenpark Square, there's a garden in the middle with parking spaces alongside the perimeter railings.'

'Yes.'

'Whereabouts were you when you were arrested?'

'Between the car and the railings.'

'And when were you first aware of this other person who was showing an interest in the car?'

'About the same time, I suppose,' he said vaguely.

Rosa sighed. Her worst fears about her client were being realised.

'Tell me the exact sequence of events from the time you walked across the road to look at the car.'

'I remember peering through the driver's window ...'

'Was that on the road or the railings side, as the car was parked?'

'The railings side.'

'So you'd walked round to its further side?'

'Yes,' he said, with a long-suffering look. 'Yes I did, if it really matters.'

'Detail is all-important in this sort of case,' Rosa retorted. 'Why were you peering through the driver's window?'

'To have a look at the instrument panel.'

'Had you walked round the front or the rear of the car?'

'The rear.'

'Yes, go on.'

'It was then I was seized by that fucking bully of a policeman. Excuse my language, but that's what he was.'

'O.K., but now you've got it off your chest, I'd sooner you didn't use that word every time you refer to him.'

He glanced at her in surprise. 'I thought you'd be used to that sort of language in your work.'

'I am, but that doesn't mean I like its gratuitous use by my clients.'

'I'll try and remember,' he said.

'Right. We've reached the point where P.C. Paynter arrested you. Where was the other man at that moment?'

'I think he was glancing into the back of the car.'

Rosa frowned as she tried, not too successfully, to visualise the scene. For the present she was content to get a general picture, though later she would need to obtain a more detailed account. Francis had already said enough, however, for her to doubt whether she was being told the whole truth or much more than a convenient approximation to it.

'Did you speak to this other person?'

'Not that I recall.'

'Surely you'd remember if you had.'

'One of us may have made a comment about the car.'

'Would you recognise him again?'

'Not a hope.'

'What sort of age was he?'

'About mine.'

'How was he dressed?'

'He could have been in yellow silk pyjamas for all I noticed.'

'I wonder why he took to his heels so smartly,' Rosa remarked thoughtfully.

'Don't ask me! He may have suddenly remembered he'd left his supper in the oven.'

'We'll have to wait and hear what the police evidence is,' Rosa remarked pointedly.

Francis scowled. 'I bet Paynter tries to verbal me.'

'Did you at any time make any sort of admission to him?'

'Of course I didn't.'

Rosa laid down her pen and read through the notes that she had made. When she looked up, she said, 'One thing I ought to say is this. It's your responsibility, as well as being very much in your interest, not to let me be

16

taken by surprise when we get to court. In brief, don't spin me any tales which are palpably false.' Without waiting for his reaction, she went on, 'Let me note down a few personal details.' After recording his date of birth and his current address, she said, 'I seem to recall Philip telling me that your parents live on the south coast.'

'My father lives at Worthing. My mother died last November.'

'I'm sorry, I didn't know . . .'

'It's all right. I haven't been home often since I left school. Since my mother's death, not at all.' There was a note of hard-crusted bitterness in his tone.

'Would you like me to get in touch with your father?'

'Good grief, no! What on earth for, anyway?'

'To find out if he's prepared to help you at a time of need.'

'He wouldn't, so that's that.' He paused before going on. 'He's over sixty and a retired Colonel. He's one of those people who believes that everyone's better for being hanged and flogged, so you don't have to be a clairvoyant to know what he thinks of me.'

'So who would speak up for you, apart from Philip, should the occasion arise?'

'You?' he said, with one eyebrow raised in wry amusement.

'I meant, as a witness.'

'I know you did. I was being flip.'

'On the whole, solicitors prefer their clients not to be flippant when they're trying to take their instructions,' Rosa said and immediately felt she had sounded unnecessarily stuffy.

'Sorry if I annoyed you.'

'You didn't annoy me, it's just that . . .'

'That I don't fit into your normal client's mould.'

'I assure that my clients don't fit into any particular mould, thank goodness!'

17

'So what is it about me that bugs you?'

'If I'm to do my best for you, the least you can do is take the case seriously. After all, it's a serious charge.'

'What? That crappy old sus law? It's a bloody scandal. Sorry, delete bloody!'

'Nevertheless, I'm sure you'd sooner not carry a conviction under it for the rest of your life.'

He gave a shrug of indifference. 'It's not likely to mar my career, if that's what you're thinking.'

'It could do at some future date,' Rosa said firmly. 'After all, you're bound to grow up sometime.'

To her surprise, he let out a laugh. 'Touché, as a friend of Philip's is always saying.'

'Well, we've made a start,' Rosa said after glancing down at her notes, 'Though I shall want much more detail from you before we go into court. In particular, detail as to what was happening in the vicinity of that car just before the police pounced. If I'm to cross-examine the officers effectively, I must have the ammunition and you're the only person who can supply it.'

'I don't know what else I can tell you,' he said in his most uninterested voice.

'Go away and think hard about it!'

'I've told you all I can.'

'Have you?'

He looked at her sharply. 'Don't you believe me then?'

'Let me put it this way. The obvious weakness of your case is that you cross the street to examine a vintage car parked in the shadows against some railings and are then arrested on its blind side where there's a second person who takes to his heels and vanishes. It's asking a lot of any court to believe you were just a couple of car enthusiasts who happened to be there at the same time.'

'I can only tell you the truth,' he said huffily.

Rosa said nothing, but privately added him to a long line

of clients whose main preoccupation was so often to conceal that peculiarly evanescent commodity from their legal adviser.

A few minutes later he had departed as he had arrived, a picture of untidy, uncouth, chip-on-shoulder youth. Even though that was the only side of him she had so far seen, she was prepared to accept that a more engaging aspect lay somewhere out of sight.

Dismissing him from her mind, she concentrated on the plea in mitigation she would have to make that afternoon. It was not until she was about to leave the office at the end of the day that he re-entered her thoughts and she decided to call Philip. But there was no reply from his flat, which was the only number she had and she resolved to try from home later in the evening.

She was putting papers into her briefcase when Robin Snaith came in and flopped into a chair.

'Who was that dubious looking young man I saw sloping out of the office just before lunch?' he asked.

'My latest client. Name of Francis Arne. Brother of Philip Arne whom I may have mentioned to you and who works for the Reynolds-Bailey Trust.'

'What's he been up to?'

'Guess!'

'Presumably not murder, robbery or rape, or he wouldn't be walking around. My bet would be drugs.'

'Section 4, Vagrancy Act. Tampering with cars. At least, that's what the police will say.'

'But your client doesn't agree?'

'Did he look the sort of person who'd agree with police evidence?'

Robin laughed. He recalled Rosa having once mentioned Philip Arne to him in a tone of voice that had set off alarm bells. It was a tone used only in respect of some of her male clients and denoted her occasional emotional vulnerability.

Rosa, so down-to-earth and excellent in every way save for this weakness. Moreover, it always seemed to be the faintly dubious young men who had the knack of stirring something within her maternal breast and Robin had come to hold his breath when he recognised the symptoms. A quick note of defiance would enter her voice should he probe. The only thing the young men had in common was age and a generally amoral attitude toward life which seemed to arouse her emotional interest.

Even though he would not have expected Francis Arne to have cast any spells over her from what he had seen of him, he was nevertheless relieved to have this confirmed by the astringent manner in which she spoke of him.

It was just after six-thirty when she parked her small Honda car outside the house on Campden Hill where she lived, and proceeded to climb the fifty-eight steps to her flat at the top. It had been her home for two years, and she still experienced a pleasurable sensation every time she unlocked her front door and stepped inside. It was her first real home and she now had the living room and her bedroom decorated and furnished as she wanted them. Those two rooms apart, there was a gleaming kitchen of built-in units and a bathroom of pale yellow, which, seeing that it had no outside window, was probably as good a colour as any. It was the original décor and she had found herself growing used to it, so that she now actually liked its lemony ambience.

As a result of Francis Arne's unheralded visit to her office that morning, she had had time for nothing more than a cup of coffee before leaving for court in the afternoon. She now realised that she was distinctly hungry.

Armed with a glass of dry white wine she went into the kitchen and set about making a cheese omelette. She took a tomato and some lettuce from the fridge and prepared a simple salad in between breaking eggs into a bowl and waiting for the butter to melt in the pan.

When the meal was ready, she put it on a tray and carried it into the living-room where she switched on the television. She usually watched whatever was on while she ate her evening meal. Later she returned to the kitchen to fetch a peach she had bought from a friendly street trader who had a stall near the office and on whom she seemed to have much the same effect as on Mr Lipstead.

By the time she had finished her meal and washed up and made herself a cup of coffee, it was nearly eight o'clock and she decided to try Philip Arne's number again. It seemed to ring endlessly and she was about to give up when the receiver was lifted and she recognised Philip's voice.

'It's Rosa Epton, Philip. I thought I'd phone and let you know how I got on with Francis this morning.'

'Can I call you later?' he said in a clearly nervous voice. 'It's a bit awkward to talk at the moment.'

'Of course. I'll be home the whole evening.'

The receiver at the other end was replaced so abruptly that Rosa felt as if a door had been slammed in her face.

When, three hours later, she went to bed, he had not returned her call. Nor had he phoned by the time she had left for the office the next morning.

One part of her said not to worry. After all, if he wasn't sufficiently interested in his brother's fate why should she bother? But against this, he had called her at home in some urgency asking to take on the defence, and had been clearly anxious about what had befallen Francis. In addition to this, there were aspects of the case she wished to discuss with Philip.

After reading her mail and dictating a number of replies, she decided to try and reach him again. This time the telephone was answered almost immediately.

'Hello,' said a soft and distinctly wary feminine voice.

21

'May I speak to Philip Arne?' Rosa said, wondering if she had the right number.

'Who's speaking?'

'Rosa Epton.'

'I'm afraid he's still asleep,' the voice said in the same soft tone. 'Perhaps you can ring later.'

The next second Rosa was cut off.

Odd, most odd, she reflected as she frowned at the instrument she was left holding in her hand.

CHAPTER 4

Police Constables Paynter and Hexham sat at a table in the corner of the deserted canteen with the air of a couple of conspirators, which, in a sense, was what they were. In the case of Peter Hexham, an extremely unhappy one. It was the first time they had got together since leaving court the previous day.

'I've written up my notes,' Paynter said, 'so you'd better make sure that yours agree. We don't want to say different things in the witness box, especially with that woman defending. Incidentally, it's enough to make you throw up the way old Lipstead runs after her with his tongue hanging out.'

He produced his pocketbook, opened it at the appropriate page and pushed it across the table at his colleague, who seemed reluctant to look at it, eventually doing so with a furrowed expression.

'I didn't actually see him try the doors of the Rolls,' he said hesitantly.

'You can't have been watching him properly then,' Paynter retorted in an uncompromising tone. 'You can take it from me that's what he did.' After a pause he added, 'And that's what we've got to say. If we don't stick together, we've had it.'

'If you're positive . . .'

'You have to be positive when you're giving evidence. Haven't you learnt that lesson yet? Once you admit you might be mistaken, you've had it. The defence just wade in and carve you up.'

'I suppose it could have been I didn't notice because I was concentrating on the other bloke.'

23

'Exactly, but you still have to back me up.' He let out a noisy sigh. 'I was bloody narked that the station sergeant wouldn't accept a charge of assault on me by Arne.'

Hexham smiled nervously. 'If anyone was assaulted, it wasn't you.'

'The essence of defence is counter-attack,' Paynter remarked, with the air of an armchair strategist. 'If that little runt takes out a summons for assault against me – which he may well do with that female defending him – I'll bloody well arrest and charge him, sergeant or no sergeant.'

'It's a pity the other bloke got away,' Hexham said gloomily.

'You made a right cock-up of that.'

'That isn't true. It was you who jumped the gun and frightened him off before I was ready.'

'No good making excuses now. And a fat lot of hope we have of ever finding him. We don't even have a decent description to put out.'

'I wonder if Arne knows who he is.'

'Of course he bloody does. I wish I could have had ten minutes alone with boyo in his cell, I'd have shaken his pal's name out of him.'

'He mayn't necessarily have known it. Could have been he was merely meeting a contact.'

'Well, whatever he knew, I'd have screwed it out of him,' Paynter said savagely. 'Now it's too late.' He undid two buttons of his tunic, leaned back and let out a noisy yawn. 'And speaking of screwing,' he went on with a leer, 'I met a nice little bit of stuff at a disco last night. Only seventeen, but not much even I could teach her. Seeing her again tonight,' he added in a tone of self congratulation. 'Incidentally, how are things going with your girl? Catherine, isn't it?'

Hexham nodded. 'She's fine,' he said abstractedly.

The truth was that he and Catherine had been going

together since just after he had joined the police and though at the beginning she had been pleased to boast about having a police constable for a boy-friend, she was becoming increasingly fretful at the unsocial hours he was obliged to work and was hinting that sooner or later he would have to choose between her and his job. The way he felt at the moment, the choice was going to be easy

He was one of those decent, pleasant-looking young men, mildly idealistic about police work, but a follower rather than a leader. In fact he was almost everything that his colleague was not.

Paynter dismissed his lecherous train of thought and refocussed his attention on his companion. The trouble with Peter Hexham and his like was that they lacked fire in their bellies. They were terrified of taking risks, and even more terrified of the consequences when they did. This made them a liability that could land everyone in trouble without it being intended. It was why Paynter was determined not to let Peter Hexham back-slide and why his face showed this in a forbidding frown. He had all the prejudices of the strata from which he came. He believed that criminals – particularly young criminals – needed nailing and that one didn't have to be too fussy how one did it. He knew there was no such thing as absolute justice and that rough and ready justice was the best anyone could, or should, expect. He affected to hold no strong political views, save that he regarded all left-wingers as a menace to his way of life and on the whole thought that the National Front had its good points.

'O.K., Pete,' he said, 'make up your notes from mine now and there won't be any slip-ups.'

While Hexham wrote, Paynter watched him with the attention of an invigilator.

Suddenly Hexham paused and frowned.

'I hadn't realised one of the keys on his ring was a skeleton one to the car doors. When did you discover that?'

'I thought I'd mentioned it,' Paynter said in an offhand tone.

'You certainly didn't.' Hexham glanced up and met his colleague's look of challenge. 'Was it really on his ring, Terry?' he asked in a worried voice.

'If that's what my pocketbook says, then it was.'

'It certainly strengthens the case against him,' Hexham said uneasily.

'Precisely.'

CHAPTER 5

Lieutenant Colonel Wilfred Arne, MC, Royal Artillery retired, had spent most of his service life in India and points east.

He had been shattered by his wife's death four months earlier, though the depths of his grief remained hidden behind the stern and unyielding façade he had always presented to the world at large.

He now stared bleakly through the french windows of the sitting-room at the rain-soaked garden beyond, which was normally maintained in immaculate military trim, but which he had let slide since his wife's death. This was now evidenced by weeds and plants that straggled like undisciplined soldiers. He told himself that, come the better weather, he would get everything shipshape again. Secretly, however, he wondered if it would be so. All his motivation seemed to have seeped away.

It was eleven o'clock and he had just tried to ring Philip's flat, but there had been no answer. He had turned away from the telephone and gone to stare moodily out of the window.

The house had been his wife's, as had the money which had converted it into a comfortable home. Now it was his, together with the rest of her property. Later it would pass to the boys in a trust which had more strings to it than a cat's cradle.

Philip had done his best to conceal his pique when he learnt the terms of his mother's will, but his father knew that he blamed *him*.

As for Francis, he had last appeared at his mother's funeral, since when his father had neither seen nor had any direct communication with him. But even before then Colonel Arne had written off his younger son like a bad debt. Moreover, he didn't have a great deal of time for much of the company kept by the older one. Though he had spent the greater part of his active life on the Indian subcontinent, he had not rubbed shoulders with the likes of many of Philip's so-called friends. His Indians had been simple, loyal folk, far removed from the smooth, venal types he had met on occasions at Philip's flat. But that was what happened, he reflected, when Asians gravitated toward a decadent, Western way of life.

Turning his back on the garden, he gazed severely round the room. As he did so, he heard Mrs Caunter, the daily help, moving in the kitchen. She was as taciturn a person as he and communication between them was kept to essentials.

Following his lunch he would spend the afternoon and early evening playing bridge at his club. He was a good player and the game was now his chief pleasure in life. Meanwhile, however, he had an hour and a half to kill before he had his lunch. He thought of getting out the car and driving to the club for a drink. But the thought was no sooner in his mind than it was dismissed.

It annoyed him that he felt so unsettled on this damp, overcast March morning. Glancing once more round the room, his eye fell on the small blank space on the wall beside his wife's chair where the Nicholas Hilliard miniature had hung. It was of an Elizabethan ancestor and had been in the family for over four hundred years. Reputedly worth ten thousand pounds, it had been of enormous sentimental value to his wife, whose wish was that it should go ultimately to the Victoria and Albert Museum for their collection.

Immediately after her death, with so many strangers constantly in and out of the house, he had removed it from display and hidden it away in a drawer. He had done the same thing with *objets d'art* that might too readily have been slipped into handbags and pockets. How ironical that now seemed!

As he stared restlessly about him he wondered whether to ring Philip's flat again, but decided it was probably pointless to do so until later in the day. Nevertheless he cast the telephone a particularly ferocious stare as if willing it to summon him. But when it remained stubbornly silent he walked briskly from the room, to return a few minutes later with a large pink gin in his hand.

Shortly afterwards the back door slammed, telling him of Mrs Caunter's departure. Though they were at pains to keep out of one another's way, he was always glad when she had gone. In about half an hour's time he would begin to savour the smell of whatever she had left for him in the oven. Till then he would quietly enjoy his drink.

Nobody could have guessed that behind the austere and disciplined exterior lurked a man near breaking point.

CHAPTER 6

Only one person in the flat where Francis Arne was living had what might be termed a regular job and he was out of the house by half past eight every morning. The others got up as their respective spirits moved them.

There was Dave who referred to himself as a painter but who had been working (his word) on the same picture for the best part of six months. He sloped about the flat yawning and scratching himself, and making endless cups of tea.

Then there was Carlos, who was a waiter and who never stirred before four in the afternoon, when he would occupy the bathroom for over an hour, leaving it smelling like a steamed up perfume factory.

But undoubtedly the most popular occupant of the flat was Perry. Popular because he was always ready to do things for others, particularly Francis. He would listen to anyone's troubles and cluck sympathetically. He would lend his clothes and even his money when he had any.

When Dave emerged from his room (or studio as he called it) around eleven o'clock that morning in search of his first cup of tea of the day, he met Perry on the landing carrying just what he wanted.

'That for me?' he asked hopefully.

'I've made it for Francis, but you can have it. I'll get him another.'

Dave took it from him and swallowed it in a few greedy gulps.

'Any chance of another?' he said holding out the empty mug. 'Anyway, why are you waiting on Francis?'

It was a foolish question to someone who waited on them

all. It was noticeable, however, that he had taken a particular shine to Francis and would follow him with doglike devotion in his eyes, slipping into his room when given half a chance.

'I'm worried about him,' Perry said. 'He came in late and was in a foul mood. He wouldn't even speak to me when I went to see if he wanted anything. It was about three o'clock and he just slammed his door and locked it in my face.'

'Locked it?' Dave said in surprise. 'Do you mean he has a lock on his door?'

Perry nodded. 'It's the only room with one.'

'It must be. Not even the loo has a lock on the door.'

Dave stared briefly at the door of Francis' room, then shrugged. 'He's probably still asleep. Why not leave him? He'll emerge when he's ready to meet life again, or bursting to have a pee.'

With Dave trailing behind him, Perry returned to the kitchen, where he was the only person ever to do any cleaning or washing-up. Armed with a second mug of tea, Dave then drifted back to his room.

'Put the kettle back on!' he called over his shoulder. 'I'll need another three or four cups before I can face the day.'

A moment or two later, Perry returned to Francis' door with a fresh mug in his hand.

'I've brought you some tea,' he called out in a cajoling tone, to be greeted only by silence. 'Please unlock the door, Francis, I want to talk to you.' But the silence continued. 'You'll feel better after a cup of tea. Please let me in. I promise not to hassle you if you want to be left alone.' He paused. 'I'll go away if you tell me to, but please say something.'

'Go away!'

It came as a muffled growl and Perry retired sadly to the kitchen, where he stood by the sink lost in thought, wondering why he always had to get involved in other people's lives. The trouble was he never felt that he had any choice in the matter. Somehow he was just sucked in. It was as if it were his appointed role in life.

CHAPTER 7

If anyone had been asked to define Shiv Kapur's duties at the Reynolds-Bailey Trust, they would have found it difficult to do so.

He's a sort of liaison officer would have been one answer, followed by *he's Philip Arne's friend and works with him.*

The trust had been founded over a hundred years ago by a Miss Alicia Reynolds-Bailey with the object of assisting Asian seamen stranded in London. During World War II it had run out of funds, but had been kept going after a fashion by a few sturdy volunteers. Since then it had become a sort of umbrella for a number of do-gooding individuals with obscure charitable aims, their only common bond being that their respective forms of benevolence were aimed at citizens of the Indian sub-continent.

Shiv Kapur was one of the people Rosa had met at Philip's party. He had been polite and charming to her, but she had been left with the feeling she wouldn't trust him even to turn off a tap. He had been with a girl whom he introduced as Nadia Beresford and who, from her expression, would have been happy to trust him ten times over with her life.

It so happened that for the past three months Nadia had shared his bed and was utterly intoxicated by everything about him. His smooth, unlined face, his rosebud mouth and mysterious little smile that he wore like a permanent buttonhole held her in thrall. Not to mention his sexual prowess and a challenging aloofness.

He accepted her protestations of devotion without ever making any similar commitment himself, the truth being that he was no more in love with her than he was with his ancestral deities. If she suddenly walked out of his life, he

33

would scarcely notice. And if he did notice, he certainly would not have gone out looking for her.

Nadia had, therefore, had to decide whether to accept him on his own terms or depart and seek solace in the arms of someone who would be no more than second best.

'You did well this morning, little Goddess,' he murmured approvingly, as he watched her slicing a mango for the fruit cocktail she was preparing for their lunch.

He had just returned to the flat in South Kensington where they lived and came straight into the kitchen, still carrying his expensive executive briefcase with its specially fitted interior.

She laid down her knife and swung round.

'Do you really mean that, my gorgeous darling?' she said eagerly.

'Of course.'

She flung her arms round his neck and kissed his soft warm mouth. He accepted the embrace with restraint and released himself when he felt that it had lasted long enough.

'It's ages since you called me little Goddess,' she said breathlessly.

'Is it?' he said, with a small distant smile.

She really was absurdly in love with him, he reflected. Even after all that had happened, basking in the warmth of his approval was all that mattered to her.

Murder had been committed, but it took second place in her thoughts. Though not in his.

CHAPTER 8

Rosa had stayed on late at the office in order to dictate a difficult brief to Counsel uninterrupted by the telephone.

She heard Robin Snaith go out, but knew he would be coming back as he always put his head round her door to say good-night before finally departing. She guessed he had slipped round to the nearby delicatessen, which was often his wont before going home to his wife and children. They lived in a charming old farmhouse which might have been miles away from anywhere apart from the fact that aeroplanes skimmed its chimney pots as they came in to land on one of Heathrow's most used runways. Having become inured to the noise over the years, the Snaiths scarcely noticed and it was their visitors who cringed and clapped their hands over their ears when sitting in the garden on a summer's afternoon.

About fifteen minutes later, Rosa heard him return and close the door of his office. A short time later, however, he came into her room carrying a newspaper.

'Have you seen an evening newspaper?' he enquired with a worried frown.

She shook her head. 'One of our clients in further trouble?' she asked, this being the usual reason for his showing her something in a newspaper.

'Read that item in stop-press,' he said gravely, handing her the paper folded at the right place.

The body of a man understood to be Philip Arne was found dead in his flat in Clapham early this afternoon. Police said he had been savagely murdered and appeared to have been dead over twelve hours.

Rosa laid the paper down and stared unseeingly across the room.

'How awful!' she said with genuine feeling. 'Who on earth could have wanted to murder him?'

'Not his brother, I hope.'

'Pray God, no. I wonder if he even knows. I ought to go and see him right away.'

'Why not call him?'

'There isn't a phone. At least, only a pay one in the main hall of the house which he says nobody ever answers. I'll drop by on my way home and find out what he knows.'

'I hope, for your sake, it's not too much. I suppose it's possible the police have already been on to him. They'll be checking on friends and family by now.'

'All the more reason for my seeing him as soon as possible,' Rosa remarked, getting up from her desk and shovelling papers into her briefcase. Noticing her partner's slightly worried expression she said, 'I'll call you at home later in the evening and tell you the score.'

'Yes, do that. I'd like to hear what you find out. Meanwhile take care, Rosa!'

'Don't I always?' she said with a quick smile.

'Almost always,' he replied with an affectionate sidelong glance in her direction.

'A qualified yes, is it? A lawyer's reply if ever I heard one,' she observed, as they exchanged grins.

It was only as she was reversing her car out of its parking place that something that should have struck her immediately now did so with hammer force.

If Philip had been dead for over twelve hours when his body was discovered, who was it who had answered the phone that morning and told her in a soothing voice that he was still asleep?

If the newspaper report was to be believed, he must already have been dead for several hours when she made her call.

36

CHAPTER 9

It was a short terraced street of porticoed houses which still bore a semblance of elegance, provided you didn't look too closely.

Rosa parked outside 24 and glanced up at the flaking paint and jagged patches where the stucco had come away.

There was a panel of bells beside the front door, but three declared themselves to be out of order and she was unable to read the name on the fourth. Not that it mattered as she had no idea what name to ask for.

She noticed that the front door was ajar and pushed it open.

Keep this door shut said a notice on its inside panel. But as soon as she closed it, it sprang open again.

The telephone in the desolate hall was ringing with the persistence of a dog barking in the night. It seemed clear that nobody was going to answer it and she walked past and began to mount the stairs. Fortunately, she recalled Francis having said he lived on the top floor of the house.

When she got there, a single door faced her and after looking for a bell or a knocker, she rapped on it with her knuckles. To her mixed surprise and relief, somebody opened it.

'Hello,' he said, 'I'm Perry. Have you come to see someone?'

He put Rosa in mind of a tame hamster. There was something friendly and engaging about him.

'Does Francis Arne live here?'

It seemed to Rosa that he deliberated before replying.

'Who shall I say wants him?' he asked at last, sounding so incongruously like a butler that Rosa let out a laugh. He

37

gave her a slightly pained look. 'What's so funny?' he said.

'It was just the way you said that. I thought you were going to turn me away because I'd not brought my calling card.'

'Oh, I see! I didn't mean to sound so pompous.'

'You didn't. It was just your choice of words ... Anyway, to answer your question, my name is Rosa Epton and I'm a solicitor. Is Francis in?'

'He's lying on his bed. I hope he's not in any trouble.'

'Could you tell him I'm here and would like to speak to him?' Rosa said, side stepping the invitation to explain the reason for her visit. She glanced past Perry along a dingy passage. 'In private, if possible.'

'I'm afraid Dave's painting in the living-room today. He says it's the only place where the light is right. Would you mind talking to Francis in his bedroom?'

'Not if he doesn't mind.'

'I'll go and tell him you're here.' He threw Rosa a faintly anxious look before scurrying away. When he reappeared, he said, 'He's in a rather funny mood. Would you like me to stay while you talk to him?'

'I'd sooner see him on my own. In what way is he in a funny mood?'

'I think something must have happened last night that upset him. He came in very late and has scarcely spoken a word since. He didn't get up till about an hour ago and then immediately went and lay down again. He's all uptight and withdrawn.'

Rosa had found her apprehension increasing with every sentence Perry uttered, but it was now too late to turn back. She had come, out of a sense of professional duty, to find out if he knew anything about his brother's death. And find out she would.

It was at that moment that she heard a door open and the object of her speculation appeared at the end of the passage.

He was wearing track suit trousers and a black sleeveless pullover, but had on neither shoes nor socks.

'Hello,' he said dully. 'Perry told me you were here.'

'I need to talk to you rather urgently, Francis,' she said.

'My bedroom's not exactly tidy, but it's the only place.' He gave her a lopsided smile. 'Don't suppose you often see your clients in their bedrooms unless it's to make their wills before they snuff it.'

'I'll be in the kitchen if you want me,' Perry said in a hopeful voice.

'You can make us some coffee,' Francis said ungraciously.

Rosa followed him into his room which was dominated by an unmade double bed. In one corner was a battered mahogany wardrobe, propped up at one end by a pile of paperbacks. The only other piece of furniture was a hard wooden chair, from the seat of which he swept off a crumpled shirt and a pair of underpants so that Rosa could sit down.

Having done this, he went and sat on the bed and swung his legs like a small boy.

'You're wondering why I've come,' Rosa said, watching him closely.

Before he could answer, however, Perry appeared at the door with two mugs of coffee, which he handed to them.

'Now shove off and shut the door behind you,' Francis said when he remained hovering just inside the room. Turning to Rosa, he added, 'Yes, I am wondering why you've come.'

'When did you last see Philip?'

Abruptly he stopped swinging his legs and gave her a suspicious stare.

'Yesterday evening, if you want to know.'

'What time?'

'About seven'

'Was that when you arrived or left?'

39

'Left. He had someone else coming and wanted me out of the way.'

'Do you know who he was expecting?'

'No idea. And in the circumstances I didn't ask him.'

'What circumstances?'

He frowned and the corners of his mouth turned down in angry recollection.

'We'd had a blazing row, if you must know.'

'What about?'

'I'm not saying.'

'Perry says you didn't come home until very late.'

'So what?'

'Where were you between leaving Philip and arriving back here?'

'What's it matter where I was?'

'It could matter a great deal.' Rosa hesitated and bit her lip. 'I didn't come here to be mysterious, but your movements last night could be of interest to the police.'

'What I did last night is no bloody business of the police,' he retorted angrily.

Rosa let out a slow sigh. She was now reasonably sure that he had no knowledge of what had happened to his brother. This was a relief to her, though she was left wondering how he would react to the news.

'I'm afraid Philip's dead,' she said quietly.

His jaw dropped and he stared at her with a painfully puzzled expression, as if trying to take in what she had said.

'I'm afraid it's true,' she went on. 'It's in this evening's paper. He's been murdered.'

He continued staring at her while a succession of emotions passed quickly across his face. Bewilderment and alarm were followed by deep thought and, Rosa felt, more than a flicker of cunning.

'Who killed him?' he said at length.

'It didn't say. I don't imagine the police have got that far.'

'I suppose you thought I might have,' he said, eyeing her dispassionately. 'That's why you asked me all those questions, wasn't it? You wanted to find out what I knew.'

'Certainly I wanted to find that out. After all, you're my professional client and your brother was a friend of mine.'

'I note the distinction,' he said with a faint note of sarcasm. 'Well, the answer's easy. I don't know anything about Philip's death. I've not been out of this room all day and nobody's shown me a newspaper.'

'Unless the police already have a line on the murderer, it's pretty certain they'll come interviewing you. And fairly soon at that.'

'You mean I'll be a suspect?' he said in a harsh tone. 'Well, they needn't try and pin Philip's murder on me because I didn't do it.' He paused. 'Though I don't suppose that'll prevent them from trying to frame me.'

'There's no reason to talk like that . . .'

'Oh, no?'

'No! Anyone who was with Philip last night will automatically be a suspect until he's eliminated. You said just now that Philip was expecting somebody after you left, but that you didn't know who. Have you no idea at all?'

He shook his head. 'None.'

'You also mentioned that you and Philip had a blazing row. What was that about?'

'I'm not saying. I didn't murder him, that's all.' He threw Rosa a suddenly suspicious look. 'The only way the police could find out that we had a row would be if you told them.'

'It's not my business to tell them,' Rosa retorted. She did have it in mind, however, that it might become her business – her civic duty – to tell them about the telephone call to Philip's flat that morning. Whoever had answered the phone obviously knew that Philip was dead at the time. She conjured up in her head once more the soft female voice that

41

had told her he was asleep.

She could only hope that representing Francis on the one hand and possibly assisting the police investigation on the other were not going to land her in any serious conflict of duty. She also wished, not for the first time, that she could feel greater confidence in anything Francis told her.

She got up and put her coffee mug down on the chair, which, apart from the floor, was the only place for it.

'If the police do come round and see you,' she said, 'tell them I'm your solicitor and you'll only talk to them in my presence.' She paused. 'Of course, if they've already made an arrest and are merely tying up the ends by interviewing family and friends, there's no reason why you shouldn't answer their questions without my presence.' She fished inside her handbag. 'Here's my home number if you want to call me.'

He took the card from her and dropped it on the bed without looking at it.

'Meanwhile,' she went on, 'you'd better think hard about what you're going to tell them about your visit to Philip's yesterday evening. After all you may have been seen coming and going by neighbours. It's even possible that your row was overheard.' She moved toward the door. 'I can see myself out,' she said pointedly when he showed no inclination to get off his bed.

'I expect Perry's hovering outside,' he observed, as he smothered a yawn.

In fact Perry was standing by the kitchen door when Rosa emerged, but his faintly guilty expression seemed to bear witness that he had overheard Francis' comment. He came forward as Rosa closed the bedroom door behind her.

'How did you find him?' he enquired anxiously, as if Rosa had been called to the bed of a sick patient.

'Much as you described,' she said dryly. 'I'm afraid I had to give him bad news. His brother's dead. He's been murdered.'

Perry's hands flew to his face.

'Oh my God!' he exclaimed. 'You don't think Francis . . .'

'He says he knows nothing about it.'

'I realised that something had upset him when he arrived back in the early hours this morning,' Perry went on in an anguished tone, as if Rosa hadn't spoken.

'But he didn't tell you anything?'

'No. Like I said to you before, he went straight to his room and locked the door. I called out and asked him if I could fetch him anything, but he wouldn't reply.'

'Was it that you happened to be up when he came in?' Rosa asked in a faintly puzzled tone.

'I was awake, listening for his return. I always worry when he's out late.' He gave her a small, shy smile. 'He's my best friend.'

And you're his doormat, Rosa thought, feeling curiously touched by such an obvious case of unrequited love.

'In what way did he appear upset?'

'He had a greenish tinge beneath his eyes.'

'Perhaps he'd been drinking,' she said, wondering how even the greenest of tinges could be distinguished from the rosiest of cheeks in that dingy passage. And at three o'clock in the morning, too!

Perry nodded. 'He does when he gets depressed.'

'Did he ever talk to you about his brother?' she asked, drawn to obtain all the information she could from his small, devoted friend.

'Not much. But then he never did talk much at all. I always gathered that Philip was the good son and that poor Francis was regarded as the black sheep. Families can be very cruel,' he added in an infinitely sad voice.

'How long have you known him?'

'Only since he's lived here, but I feel it's much longer than that.'

They had been standing by the front door and Rosa had

43

thought it probable that Francis must be aware they were talking about him.

'I ought to be going,' she said abruptly. 'I'm glad I met you.'

Perry threw her a grateful look. 'Is there anything I can do to help?' he asked. 'I'd do literally anything for him.'

'Nothing at the moment, Perry. Perhaps later.'

As she drove away, she pondered the next step. Maybe she would find out the name of the officer in charge of the murder enquiry. If it was somebody she knew – and got on with – it would make things easier.

She increasingly felt that it would be her duty to tell the police of her phone call to Philip's flat that morning. The fact that it was certainly not Francis who had answered, plus his seeming innocence of the crime, made her decision that much easier. And even if he should fall under suspicion, what she had to tell the police couldn't aggravate his position. On the contrary it might help to eliminate him as a suspect that much sooner.

Accordingly, as soon as she got home, she would make the necessary phone calls.

CHAPTER 10

Detective Chief Inspector Tom Sweet matched his name, being a generally friendly and benevolent man. Now in his forty-first year with thinning, honey-coloured hair and a waistline with which he was constantly at war, he reckoned to enjoy the greater part of his life. The trouble was, so far as his weight was concerned, that he enjoyed all the things that spelt poundage and detested the insipid diets into which his wife pushed him from time to time. He knew he could never look slim, but he did try and avoid the appearance of an over-inflated gourd.

He had risen steadily up the promotional ladder and might yet make it to Detective Superintendent. On the other hand, he wasn't sure that he hadn't had enough of the police. The unsocial hours and the utter dedication that was called for made him wonder whether any job was worth it. He was not the complaining sort, but he had more or less decided to take early retirement and get one of those attractive security posts with a good salary, a company car and other desirable perks which had become the target of every retiring police officer of seniority.

He had been half way through a plate of his wife's best steak and kidney pie (she had relented that day) when he had been called to the scene of Philip Arne's murder. It was not often that he got home for lunch and he felt a bit like Sir Francis Drake on the approach of the Spanish Armada, except instead of a game of bowls to be finished, it was an apple crumble to be tackled after the steak and kidney pie. Habit and a sense of duty, however, got him up from the table and within two minutes of the call he was on his way.

Three police cars were already at the scene and there were small clusters of curious bystanders on the pavements. A reporter from a South London paper stood impatiently at the gate, kept at bay by a young constable whose handset crackled with mysterious noises that could have been coming from outer space.

It was one of those London streets that was distinctly down market at one end, but with expensively and trendily converted houses at the other. It was in one of these that Philip Arne had the top floor flat.

Chief Inspector Sweet hurried inside and, despite the steak and kidney pie which was still being processed by his digestive juices, ran up the carpeted stairs, arriving at the top flushed and tiresomely breathless.

He was greeted at the flat's front door by Detective Sergeant Adderly who remarked cheerfully, 'You've got here jolly quickly, sir. And you came up those stairs like a gazelle.'

Paul Adderly was an efficient young C.I.D. officer who found it difficult to repress his perkiness. Sweet had more than once felt obliged to caution him against a habit which irritated many of his superiors. Privately, he thought his sergeant would either end up as a chief constable or nosedive out of the force before he was much older.

'Watch out where you tread, sir,' Adderly said over his shoulder as he led the way into the flat. 'There are more blood-stains around than you'd find in a slaughter-house. They're all dry now, but as forensic haven't yet been, I've told everyone to mind their step.' He paused in the doorway of the living-room and stood aside so that his chief inspector could look in. 'There he is. Dead over twelve hours according to Dr Blair. The pathologist should be here any minute. It'll probably be Dr Murphy.'

'Who discovered the body?' Sweet asked, after glancing round the room with a professional eye.

'Dr Blair whom I've just mentioned. He and his wife live

46

in the flat below. Actually it was his wife who made the discovery. They'd been away overnight and came back about eleven o'clock this morning. Mrs Blair noticed a nasty reddy brown stain on their bedroom ceiling. She drew her husband's attention to it and he immediately realised it had been caused by seeping blood. He came up here and when he couldn't get any answer, he phoned the police.'

'Where were they spending the night?' Sweet enquired.

'I thought you'd ask that, sir. What's a G.P. doing away from home, I also asked myself? The answer is that he always takes off Thursday afternoons and he and his wife go and spend the evening at his married daughter's in North London and stop the night. That way he ensures he can't be reached on the phone. His partners know where he is, but nobody else.' He paused and went on in the same pleased tone, 'I know what you're thinking, sir. That the victim presumably knew of this piece of routine and quite possibly the murderer as well. *Ipso facto,* if you're going to commit a murder in the top flat, Thursday evening's the time to do it.'

Sweet had not, in fact, been thinking anything of the sort, but couldn't be bothered to say so. He merely stood there, his nostrils twitching slightly.

'Joss sticks,' Adderly said, with the air of an eager young salesman.

'What are you on about now?'

'Joss sticks, sir. You know, a sort of Chinese incense. You burn them. That's what you can smell. As a matter of fact, the whole flat is full of oriental bric a brac, mostly Indian stuff. Even the murder weapon.' He pointed at the floor beside the dead man's head. 'It's a nine inch bronze of an Indian Goddess. Lakshmi, bride of Vishnu, if I'm not mistaken.'

'I'm all too certain you're not,' Sweet said in a tone of mild exasperation. 'But how the hell do you know?'

Sometimes, working with Sergeant Adderly was like having a guided tour of a museum.

'My uncle has one exactly like it,' Adderly went on. 'He bought it in Madras at the end of World War Two. It's probably about a hundred years old.' He gave Sweet a side-long glance to see how his discourse was being received and decided to revert to practicalities. 'It was obviously gripped by its head and wielded like a hammer. And with enormous ferocity, too. You observe that the victim's head has been smashed in.'

'So I can see,' Sweet remarked drily.

'Incidentally, the dead man's name is Philip Arne.'

'That's one thing I did know before I arrived.'

'He worked for something called the Reynolds-Bailey Trust which was originally established to help the Indian community.'

'Originally? But not any longer, are you saying?' Sweet said, sensing an opportunity to discountenance his sergeant.

'No, I'm not actually saying that, sir. I'm afraid I don't know the scope of its present activities.'

Sweet raised a mildly mocking eyebrow and Adderly gave him a sheepish grin.

'I was still in the process of information-gathering when you arrived, sir.'

Sweet gave a tiny nod and smiled to himself. It was occasionally necessary to quell his sergeant's cockiness.

'Did Arne live here on his own?'

'I gather from the Blairs that he often had different girls who stopped the night.'

'What about his family?'

'I'm trying to trace a younger brother who sounds like a bit of a drop-out and who used to visit here quite often. Most of his friends appear to have been Indian.'

'Parents?'

'I've not yet found out anything about them.'

'Did you ask the Blairs?'

'Yes, but they weren't really on social terms with Arne and.couldn't help.'

Sweet glanced round the room until his gaze alighted on a desk in the farther corner.

'Anything interesting there?' he enquired, with a slight note of malice.

'I can't say, sir,' Adderly replied, adding in a slightly huffed voice, 'I only arrived here about forty minutes before you. I've not had time to examine everything.'

'That's all right, I only asked. It'll give me something to do while we're waiting for forensic and Dr Murphy to turn up.'

'I *have* had a look round his bedroom,' Adderly said in a clear attempt to restore his self-esteem. 'The bed had not been slept in last night and there was no sign of any disorder. Apart from this room and the bedroom, there's only a kitchen and a bathroom.'

Having already worked this out for himself, Sweet's only response was a grunt.

'Any sign of blood in the bathroom?'

'No, sir.'

'Nevertheless, we'll get forensic to remove the basin and bath waste pipes for examination. It's inconceivable that the murderer left without having a wash, which means there could still be blood somewhere in the plumbing system.'

Stepping farther into the room, he stood for a full half-minute peering down at the body.

Philip Arne was lying on his front with his head turned slightly to the left, revealing a mass of dark caked blood and some brain tissue which had exuded from a wide gash running from the crown of his head down behind the left ear. His legs were outstretched and his arms were flung out as if groping for something beyond his reach. He was wearing a

49

pair of jeans and a black T-shirt. On his feet was a pair of sandals.

'My guess would be,' Sweet said, 'that he was felled from behind and then subjected to further blows as he lay on the ground.' He glanced about him. 'I wonder where this statue thing normally rested. Possibly at the end of that bookcase.' He stepped across and examined the top of a bookcase which ran half the length of one wall. 'Yes, one can see from the dust marks exactly where it must have been.'

'Everything points to the murderer being known to his victim,' Adderly said in his most sententious voice.

'I don't doubt it,' Sweet remarked. Turning to his sergeant, he went on, 'I want to have details of all the comings and goings in this house during the course of yesterday evening. Neighbours must have seen or heard something.'

'I already have that in train, sir.'

'Good.'

'I've got officers making door-to-door calls,' he added in a self-satisfied tone.

'Who else lives in this house apart from Dr and Mrs Blair?'

'A Mr and Mrs Naunton live on the ground floor. He works for an oil company and spends a lot of time abroad. In fact, he's in the Middle East at the moment. Mrs Naunton is a schoolteacher and a local councillor and didn't get home until after midnight following a lengthy council meeting. She says she didn't hear any sounds coming from upstairs and is certain nobody left the house after she arrived back. She says she's a light sleeper and the slightest noise wakes her.'

Sweet permitted himself another grunt. In his experience, people were apt to be surprisingly self-deceptive about their sleeping habits.

'The murderer may have crept out very quietly,' he said.

Sergeant Adderly pursed his lips. 'In my view, sir, it's almost impossible to leave a house in the stillness of the night without making some noise. Stairs creak. Doors have to be closed. Particularly the front door which would require to be pulled against the catch.'

'The murderer may have a key.'

'I suppose it's a possibility, sir . . .'

'Anyway, who owns the house?'

'An Indian named Shiv Kapur. He's a friend of Arne's. I gather they work together. Mrs Blair says he's a very Westernised person and apparently an excellent landlord. Has plenty of money, too, by the sound of him. He lives somewhere in the South Ken area and I'm having him traced now.'

Sweet let out another non-committal grunt. 'If he's a friend of Arne's, his address is probably somewhere in this room.'

'As I've said, sir,' Adderly replied with a return of his huffed tone, 'I haven't had time to search the whole place.'

'I know. You've not done too badly, so cheer up.'

Sergeant Adderly gave his chief inspector a wry grin and watched him pick his way carefully over to the corner where the desk sat.

Chief Inspector Sweet regarded people's desks as being the repositories of all manner of information useful to a police investigation. What was not relevant could often be eye-opening.

Philip Arne's desk, however, turned out to be as un-informative as the day it left the factory. As Sweet went from drawer to drawer his suspicion grew that somebody had been there ahead of him and removed everything that might have interested the police. By the time he finished, the suspicion had become a near certainty.

There were some unpaid household bills in a pigeon hole and next to them an unused cheque book from which he could, at least, take details of Arne's bank account. But there

51

wasn't a single personal letter, nor yet an address book or diary.

Either Philip Arne had been careful not to keep anything that might provide a clue to his personal life (and that in itself was perhaps significant) or, as Sweet was now firmly of the opinion, somebody had removed every scrap of evidence that Philip Arne ever had a private life. And who could that have been but the murderer?

It was while he was still over by the desk that Sergeant Adderly returned to the room.

'Any luck, sir?'

Sweet shook his head and voiced his suspicions.

'That could tie up with what I've just learnt, sir. Apparently, a Mrs Donnington who lives in the house opposite has told P.C. Arkwright that she saw a girl leaving here about ten o'clock this morning. She says it wasn't Mrs Naunton whom she knows by sight and it couldn't have been Mrs Blair because they didn't get back until eleven. She describes her as a girl in her early to mid-twenties.'

'Well, go on,' Sweet said when Adderly paused.

'I'm afraid that's all she's able to say. You see, the girl was wearing some sort of duffle coat with the hood covering her head, so that Mrs Donnington never got a proper look at her face.'

'How does she know her age then?' Sweet asked suspiciously.

'I imagine from the girl's general appearance, sir.'

'She may have been a sprightly fifty-year-old. It may even have been a transvestite.'

Adderly smiled perfunctorily. 'I doubt it, sir. Anyway, it's something to work on.'

'It'd be easier to look for a needle in a haystack,' Sweet grumbled.

By the time he left the flat some two hours after his arrival, he had been formally told what had been obvious all along, namely that Philip Arne had died as a result of multiple fractures of the skull. Dr Murphy, the pathologist, timed his death as having taken place some fifteen to nineteen hours previously which put it between eight p.m. and midnight the previous day. Experts from the Forensic Science Laboratory had been and gone, taking with them a collection of samples for detailed examination. But the mysterious girl in the duffel coat was no closer to being identified.

On the credit side, he now had the address of Shiv Kapur, landlord and reputed friend of the dead man.

It was not until later that day he traced the whereabouts of Francis Arne and about the same time, received a message to the effect that a solicitor named Rosa Epton had certain information she wished to impart to the police.

He had met Rosa when he had been a detective inspector on another division. He regarded her as a tough but honest opponent in court and as a pleasant woman outside it. He had early on learnt that a small, elfin-like girl was not necessarily a pushover in the field of forensic combat.

When he lifted the receiver of his telephone to return her call, he did so with a mixture of interest and hope.

He didn't expect her to hand him the name of the murderer on a plate, but any offer of information was more than welcome, for a murder enquiry without a flow of information was like a riverbed without water.

CHAPTER 11

'Miss Epton? This is Detective Chief Inspector Sweet. I received your message when I got back a short while ago. I'm delighted to hear you're in a position to help my enquiry. As you know, we can never have too much.'

'I understand from a newspaper report, Mr Sweet, that Philip Arne was murdered last night. It so happens I called him about eight o'clock and he asked if he could ring me back, but he never did. He sounded a bit fraught and said it was awkward to talk then. As I'd heard nothing further I called him again just before ten this morning and a girl answered and told me he was still asleep and would I try later.' Rosa paused and went on. 'In case you're wondering, Mr Sweet, why I was calling him, it was about his younger brother whom I'm defending on a charge at Shepherd's Bush Magistrates' Court. I knew Philip and in fact it was he who asked me to represent his brother.'

'That's most interesting and helpful, Miss Epton,' Sweet said when she had finished. 'It also ties up with other information, namely that a girl was seen leaving the house where he lives about ten o'clock this morning. Did you by any chance recognise her voice?'

'No.'

'Might you, if you heard it again?'

'Possibly.'

'You realise we'll need to interview your client.'

'Of course, but I should like to be present.'

'I never said he was a suspect, Miss Epton.'

'You also never said he wasn't. Moreover, he did visit his brother last night. He left because Philip said he was expecting someone else.'

54

'What time was that?'

'Around seven.'

'Is there independent proof of that?'

Rosa hesitated. 'I'm certain it'll be forthcoming,' she said boldly.

'And who was the dead man expecting?'

'He didn't tell his brother.'

There was a silence before Sweet said in a slightly depressed voice, 'Has it occurred to you, Miss Epton, that you could find yourself in the embarrassing position of being a witness for the prosecution at the same time as you're representing the defendant? It would be an impossible conflict of interest.'

'I agree. But it won't arise because my client didn't murder his brother.'

'You sound very confident about that.'

'I am.'

'Well, I'm very grateful to you for your information.' He paused. 'How would you like to bring your client to the station in about an hour's time?'

'Tonight, you mean?'

'Yes. If it's not convenient for you to come, I'll send a car to pick him up, but the sooner I see him the better.'

'No, I'll bring him,' Rosa said quickly.

She realised that Sweet had made the offer to her in return for the information she had given him. But supposing Francis wasn't there when she went round! Supposing he had already done a bunk! Well, she would have to deal with that situation, if it arose, as best she could.

Reviewing in her mind what she had told Chief Inspector Sweet, she still felt she had done the right thing. It would have been wrong, however, to have told the police of the row Francis had had with his brother and she had not done so. On the other hand she had certainly stuck her neck out when she had confidently said she was sure there would be confirmation forthcoming of the hour Francis had left his brother's flat. After all, he had refused to tell her what the row had been about and also how he had spent the remainder of the evening.

She realised in retrospect that she had taken some risks not only on his behalf, but also on her own.

But then calculated risks were part of her business.

She glanced at her watch. It was a few minutes before nine. With a sigh she gathered up her coat and handbag and made sure she had the materials for note-taking in her brief-case.

CHAPTER 12

'Live on your own, do you, Mr Kapur?' Sergeant Adderly
enquired with studied casualness, as he surveyed the huge
double bed in a room that was all white apart from the midnight blue ceiling which was decorated with silver stars and
half-moons.

'From time to time,' Shiv Kapur replied equably with a
placid smile. 'But come into the living-room and let me
fetch you a drink. I would guess you're a Scotch man.'

'I shouldn't drink at all on duty, but I wouldn't say no to a
beer.'

'Certainly. I can offer you four varieties. Lager, Guinness,
Pale Ale and a special export beer brewed for countries with
religious susceptibilities about drinking. Which will you
have?'

'A pale ale, please.'

Shiv Kapur had deemed it courteous to offer his visitor
Scotch as a first choice, though fairly certain that he would
opt for beer.

'It is very sad news that you bring,' he said, as he handed
Adderly his beer and poured himself an orange juice. 'Very
distressing indeed. Apart from the fact that Philip was my
dear friend, that he should die in such a manner is terrible.'

'And on your property,' Adderly chipped in.

'That, too.'

'When did you last see him?'

'Two days ago. He came in for a visit during the evening.
Just a social occasion, you understand.'

'Why should I not understand that?'

Shiv Kapur let out a small giggle. 'Quite so. What I meant
was that though we originally met professionally, all our

57

recent contact has been delightfully social.'

'Tell me something about the Reynolds-Bailey Trust where you both worked.'

'It was established to assist Indian seamen who found themselves in this country without resources through no fault of their own.' He gave a small deprecating smile. 'Well, perhaps I shouldn't put it quite like that because quite often their lack of resources was their own fault, as they had gambled or drunk their money away. The Trust now concerns itself more with the welfare of immigrants to this country from the sub-continent. I don't have to tell *you*, a detective sergeant in the world's most famous police force, how great is their need for advice and help.'

'And what exactly was Mr Arne's function?'

'Apart from taking a great and compassionate interest in individual cases, he was a vital liaison man.'

'Did he have many Indian friends?'

'Very, very many. They all loved him. He had no racist feeling whatsoever. There'll be much grief at his tragic death.'

'Did he have any enemies you know of?'

'Certainly not amongst the Indian community,' Shiv Kapur said, with a sorrowful shake of his head.

'So you don't think we'll find his murderer there?'

'No. There isn't one who'd have harmed him.' He paused. 'May I be permitted to ask how he was killed?'

'I wondered if you were going to.'

Kapur gave a small shrug. 'It is you, detective sergeant, who is conducting this interview and putting the questions. I did not wish to seem presumptuous by showing unwelcome curiosity.'

'His head was smashed in with a bronze statue.'

'Lakshmi?'

'You know the statue then?'

'I gave it to him. It is Lakshmi in the cow tail's stance; the cow being a sacred animal in India.' Kapur turned his head aside and appeared to blink away some tears. 'That makes it terribly worse,' he said. Then fixing Adderly with an expression of infinite sadness, he went on, 'It also proves conclusively he couldn't have been killed by an Indian. None of my people would have desecrated the image of the holy Goddess in such a way. It is sacrilege. Whoever did it will surely be punished for his wickedness.'

'Let's hope so,' Adderly murmured, glancing thoughtfully about the room.

All the social workers he knew lived sparsely. If not wholly indigent, they certainly didn't enjoy the sort of trappings on display in Shiv Kapur's flat.

'You have a very nice place here, Mr Kapur,' he remarked.

'I think I can read your thoughts, detective sergeant,' Kapur said in a voice that carried a note of mild reproach.

'I come from a wealthy family. I also have a social conscience. Put the two together and you have the explanation of my comfortable home and of my unpaid work for the Reynolds-Bailey Trust.'

Sergeant Adderly nodded sagely. 'Some would say you're a lucky man, Mr Kapur.'

'I can't deny it. I'm blessed in many ways.'

'Tell me, do you have a set of keys to Mr Arne's flat?'

'I have a key to the main door of the house, but not to individual flats.' He made a small grimace. 'My tenants would not otherwise be very happy.'

'Some landlords do, of course, retain keys to the flats they rent out.'

'But I am not one of them.' For once the tone was sharp and Adderly wondered at the reaction he had got.

'Did Philip Arne live alone?'

'He had many girl-friends.'

'That doesn't exactly answer my question.'

59

'I am not my brother's keeper.'

'Nor does that! Who's his current girl-friend?'

'I am not aware of any current girl-friend, as you put it,' Kapur said with a note of asperity. 'I am sorry, but with my friend tragically dead, I do not find it easy to talk so lightly about such things as his love life.'

'That may be your privilege, Mr Kapur, but it's not mine. The police can't show the same sort of delicate feeling when they're investigating a murder. However, as far as you're aware, he didn't have anybody, girl or boy, living with him at the present time, is that right?'

Kapur let out one of his surprising giggles. 'Never a boy. Philip was not one of them.'

'It wouldn't have mattered to me if he had been. It so happens, Mr Kapur, you're looking on that rare bird, a police officer without any racial, social or sexual prejudices.'

'I congratulate you. You are obviously a particularly broad-minded and intelligent detective sergeant.'

Adderly accepted the encomium with a shrug, not to indicate his disagreement with it so much as to deplore the failure of his own superiors to accord him similar recognition.

'So,' he said with the air of a chairman of a panel discussion, 'if Philip Arne wasn't murdered by one of your fellow countrymen, who do you think might have killed him? I can't believe you don't have some ideas on the subject.'

'Alas, detective sergeant, I cannot help you. I, too, am mystified that anyone could have wished to murder Philip. He didn't have an enemy in the world.'

'If that's true, he was a lucky man. But I know what you mean.' After a slight pause, he added, 'What about his brother, Francis?'

Shiv Kapur once more assumed his sorrowful expression. 'A nice boy, but unstable. Philip was always very good to him; always helping him out of trouble.'

'What sort of trouble?'

'He had a passion for cars. Other people's cars, I'm afraid.'

'I take it you're referring to trouble with the police?'

Kapur gave the merest nod. 'I don't know any details because Philip was very loyal and didn't like talking about it.'

'Nevertheless, what you're telling me in a subtle way is that Francis Arne might have murdered his brother?'

'Please, detective sergeant, I said no such thing.'

'But you implied it.'

'Not that!'

'I think you did.'

'No, no! It's not for me to sow any suspicions in your mind.'

'Of course not,' Adderly said with a grin.

It was a few minutes later when he was about to leave that he made an excuse to go into the bathroom where he confirmed what he had believed all along. Namely that Shiv Kapur had a resident girl-friend. He wondered who and where she was. It was now half past eight in the evening and one might have expected her to be home. It seemed likely, however, that she was being kept out of the way until he had departed.

'I like your girl-friend's taste in bath-oil,' he said with a knowing smile as he emerged.

'Then I must give you some for your birthday,' Kapur remarked blandly. There was a glitter in his eyes, however, that told a different story.

CHAPTER 13

Francis didn't seem particularly surprised to see Rosa when she arrived to take him to the police station.

She explained what had happened while he listened to her in scowling silence. He picked up his leather jacket from the floor beside his bed and put it on.

'O.K., I'm ready,' he said laconically.

Rosa, nevertheless, had the impression he was glad of her company on this occasion.

'Only two words of advice,' she said when they were in the car, 'try not to upset Sweet unnecessarily . . .'

'Supposing he upsets me?'

'Swallow hard and count up to ten before you say anything.'

'I'd better make it twenty,' he said with one of his rare smiles. 'And what's the second word of advice?'

'Don't tell him anything that can immediately be disproved.'

'Such as?'

'That you went from Philip's flat to the Savoy Hotel where you'd booked a table for dinner in the grill-room. And on the subject of that, you still haven't told me where you did spend the time between leaving Philip's flat and arriving home at three in the morning. That's almost eight hours unaccounted for.'

He was silent for a while before replying. 'I suppose you'll have to know sooner or later. I spent most of it at a club called The Tunnel. It's in Soho. Naughty things go on there,' he added, giving her a sidelong glance.

'How naughty?'

'Rampant sex, you might say.'

'Men and women, you mean?'

'Good God, no! Men and men. I thought you realised I was that way. Though as a matter of fact I also sleep with the occasional girl. I even carry a picture of my last girl-friend in my wallet. It saves tiresome explanations.'

Rosa frowned. 'How do you mean?'

'Such as when you're arrested and the police pick through your possessions.'

'I see what you mean. Anyway, your sex life is no business of mine. Can anyone confirm that you were at the Tunnel Club last night?'

'The barman can if he wants to. I spent quite a while drinking at the bar.'

'Anybody else there who might remember you?'

'It isn't exactly a place where people are remembered by their faces.'

'Well, it's very important we can establish your alibi.'

'Except that the police will automatically disbelieve anyone from there.'

'Do the police know what goes on at the club?'

'If they're half as bright as they pretend, they must do.'

'But they turn a blind eye for some reason, is that what you're suggesting?'

'Your guess is as good as mine.'

'What time did you arrive at and leave the club?'

'I was there from roughly ten-thirty until two. I then walked home and it took a good hour.'

'So where were you between seven and ten-thirty?'

'Wandering the streets. I stopped for a drink in a pub behind Leicester Square and spent about half an hour there.'

'Alone?'

'Yes, but the barmaid knows me. She'll say I was there.'

'The important thing about any alibi is that it's completely watertight. We'll need to make sure that yours is.'

'Isn't that what lawyers are for? To fix their clients up with alibis.'

'I don't know if that remark was intended to be offensive, but it certainly was.'

'I thought there were lawyers who did do that.'

'There probably are, but I'm not one of them. I don't fabricate evidence on behalf of my clients. I just do my best with what's given to me.'

'Anyway, I didn't murder my brother,' he said, 'so the police can stuff it.'

'Remember what I said about not rubbing Sweet up the wrong way.'

'You can kick me under the table when you see the danger signs.'

'Better still, don't manifest any!' Rosa pulled out to over-take a bus and didn't speak again until the manoeuvre was completed. 'Are you yet prepared to tell me why you had a row with Philip last night?'

He was silent for a few seconds, then shook his head. 'No! As I didn't kill him, it's not relevant.' In what Rosa took to be a placatory tone, he went on, 'I may tell you later, but I promise you it had no bearing on his death. As I didn't murder him, it couldn't have had.'

Rosa believed him but wondered why, seeing that she doubted his word on so much else. Perhaps it was to do with Philip's apparent affection for his younger brother and her desire to believe it was a two-way feeling. Before she had time to pursue her thoughts further on the subject, they arrived at the police station.

Sweet greeted Rosa with a tired smile and formally shook hands with Francis.

'I understand from Miss Epton that you visited your brother yesterday evening, Mr Arne, is that correct?'

'Yes.'

To Rosa's sensitive ears, the monosyllable seemed to carry

an incipient note of truculence, which Sweet appeared to disregard.

'What time did you arrive at his flat?'

Francis swallowed. 'About six o'clock,' he said with a bored shrug.

'And when did you leave?'

'About an hour later.'

'Say seven o'clock?'

'Yes.'

'Might you have left later than that?'

'No. Philip was expecting someone and wanted me out of the way.'

'Is that what he said?'

'Yes.'

'Did he say whom he was expecting?'

'No.'

'And you didn't ask?'

'No.'

'And you've no idea at all?'

'None.'

'What was the object of your visit?'

'It was just a social visit.'

'I believe you'd seen your brother earlier in the day at Shepherd's Bush Magistrates' Court?'

'Yes. It was then he suggested I should go round for a drink that evening. Come at six, he said.'

'Did he mention that you could only stay an hour as he was expecting someone else later?'

'No.'

'How long were you expecting to stay when you arrived?'

'It depended on him. Sometimes he'd throw me out, saying he had work to do. Other times we'd go out to the Chinese takeaway and I'd spend the rest of the evening with him.'

'Had he ever thrown you out before because he had somebody coming?'

'Quite often he'd have meetings at the flat and tell me I'd have to go.'

'What sort of meetings?'

'To do with his work, I imagine.'

'Was this the first time he'd asked you to leave without giving you a proper explanation?'

'He did give me a proper explanation. He had somebody coming.'

'And you never asked who that somebody was?'

'No.'

'During the hour you spent with him, did he appear to be his normal self?'

'Yes.'

And yet by eight o'clock when Rosa spoke to him, he was most definitely not his normal self, she reflected, and could tell that the same thought was passing through Sweet's mind.

'What did you talk about?'

'Nothing in particular,' Francis said with an impatient shrug.

'I'd have thought you might have discussed your court appearance that morning,' Sweet persisted.

'I think that did come up, yes.'

'After all, it was your brother who secured Miss Epton's services for you.'

'I know.'

'What was his attitude toward your being charged?'

'He said he'd help me.'

'That all he said?'

Rosa decided she ought to intervene. 'If you're going to question my client about his current court case, I shall need to advise him,' she said firmly.

Sweet sighed. 'I don't really want to question him about it

at all. I just want to get a picture of this hour he and his brother spent together last night. After all, at the moment your client was the last person to have seen his brother alive.'

'Apart from the murderer, you mean,' Rosa remarked.

Sweet nodded thoughtfully. Turning back to Francis he said, 'Did you have a drink while you were at his flat?'

'I had a glass of wine.'

'Did he have one, too?'

'Yes.'

'Did he appear to have anything on his mind?'

'No-o.'

'He didn't exhibit any signs of anxiety?'

'No.'

'All he said was that he was expecting somebody else and wanted you out of the way before they arrived?'

'Yes.'

'At what stage did he tell you that?'

'Not long before he pushed me out,' Francis said vaguely. 'Yes, I remember now. He suddenly said, you'll have to go. I've got somebody coming and I don't want you here when they arrive.'

Rosa listened with an impassive expression as she tried to make up her mind how much of her client's story she actually believed. Of one thing she was quite sure. If Chief Inspector Sweet learnt that the two brothers had had what Francis had referred to as a blazing row, the interview would be taking a very different course. It was her knowledge of that row she found inhibiting. What had they quarrelled about? And why wouldn't Francis tell her?

She had no complaint about the way Sweet had so far conducted the interview and her impression was that he was keeping an open mind as to what had happened. He obviously had no evidence against Francis. On the other hand, it would be surprising if he were ready to eliminate him from the investigation on the strength of what

Francis had told him this evening.

'What did you do after leaving your brother's flat?' Sweet now asked.

'I walked all the way to a pub near Victoria and went in and had a drink.'

'That's quite a walk.'

'I often walk in London at night. I enjoy it.'

'What was the name of the pub?'

'The Royal Arms.'

'Can anyone vouch for your presence there?'

'There's a blonde barmaid called Marita. She knows me.'

'How long did you spend there?'

'About an hour. From around eight until nine.'

'And after that?'

'I went to another pub near Leicester Square.'

'And then?'

'I wandered round the Piccadilly area, ending up at a club I know.'

'Can you tell me the name?'

Francis pursed his lips and Rosa wondered if he was going to stall.

'It's the Tunnel Club in Soho, if you must know,' he said with a note of defiance.

'Never heard of it,' Sweet said mildly. 'Recommend it for a night out with my wife?' Francis scowled nervously and Sweet went on, 'How long did you stay there?'

'Till around two o'clock. Then I walked home.'

'Another long walk, Soho to Hammersmith!'

'I've told you, I walk a lot at nights.'

'I ought to do more of it. Walking, that is. It's the best form of exercise when you reach my age.' He seemed to shake himself from a reverie and, refocussing his gaze on Francis, said, 'So you never returned to you brother's flat after leaving it at seven o'clock?'

'Definitely not.'

'When did you first hear he was dead?'

'Miss Epton came round to where I live and told me this evening.'

'Well, I think that's about all for the time being, Mr Arne. I'll want you to sign a statement incorporating what you've told me. I'm sure Miss Epton will advise you that's normal procedure. I'll need to see you again to tie up loose ends, but when will depend on how my investigation goes. I'm hoping we'll get a break and make an early arrest. Incidentally, what's your family consist of?'

'There was just my brother and me.'

'Parents alive?'

'My father is.'

'Have you been in touch with him about your brother's death?'

'No.'

The message was loud and clear and Sweet said, 'I'd better get the local police to inform him. Can you give me his address?'

Francis did so in a voice that was cold and detached, as if to underline his feelings toward his father.

They were both silent as Rosa drove him home until just before they reached the house.

'I should have asked you this before,' she said, 'but have you any previous convictions?'

He shook his head.

'That makes life easier,' she added with a faint smile.

He threw her a sidelong glance. 'Though that's not the fault of the police.'

'You'd better explain.'

'About a year ago I was hauled up in court and charged with taking away someone's car without their consent. It was all a crazy mix-up and the charge would never have been brought if the police hadn't been so officious.'

'I take it you were found not guilty?'

'You may put it like that. I'm saying I was found innocent.'

Rosa nodded. She was too tired to join issue with him over such legal niceties. She found it hard to realise that it was less than forty-eight hours ago Philip Arne had called her. It seemed more like a decade. It had been a call that had set off a train of utterly unforeseen events, which were still running their hectic course without an end in sight.

Somehow she was sure that Philip's murder and his brother's appearance in court were connected, but for the moment both events seemed obscured by mists of swirling doubt and half-hidden truth.

All she knew for certain was that she was filled with a sense of foreboding.

CHAPTER 14

It fell to Police Constable Fox to visit Colonel Arne and break the news to him of his son's death.

In carrying out this melancholy duty the police invariably show great tact and sympathy and P.C. Fox was renowned for his bedside manner.

When he telephoned in advance of his visit he was told that the colonel was out but would be back within half an hour. On enquiring politely whether he was speaking to Mrs Arne, he was brusquely informed that the colonel was a widower and it was his housekeeper who was speaking.

When he arrived at the house, however, the door was opened by the colonel himself.

'I don't like talking to people on my doorstep, so you'd better come in,' he said in an uncompromising tone.

'Thank you, sir,' Fox said, solemnly removing his helmet as if going into a place of worship.

His host marched ahead of him into the living-room and went and stood with his back to the fireplace.

'Sit down if you wish. I suppose you've come about the accident I reported the other day.'

Fox, who had lowered himself rather gingerly on to one of the more upright chairs (he was a large man and chairs were apt to let out protesting creaks when he sat on them), shook his head.

'No, sir, about your son. I'm afraid I have bad news for you.'

'Bad news? Which of my sons are you talking about?'

Fox consulted his pocketbook.

'Mr Philip Arne, sir. I'm very sorry to have to tell you that he's dead.' It seemed to Fox that the colonel's bleak expression showed no change at the news.

'I regret to say, sir, that he's been found murdered.'

'When was this?' the colonel's tone was sharp as if he were questioning an out-of-breath messenger on the field of battle.

'I understand, sir, that the police were called to his flat in Clapham yesterday afternoon. He had apparently been dead for several hours. They weren't able to trace you as his next of kin until last night and, owing to a bit of a slip-up, we weren't asked to let you know until this morning. Most regrettable, sir,' Fox murmured apologetically.

But Colonel Arne brushed the apology aside with an impatient gesture.

'Has anyone been arrested yet?' he enquired as soon as P.C. Fox had rumbled to a halt.

'I gather not, sir, but I'm sure it won't be long before they get a lead. It always takes a bit of time to analyse the clues. That is, unless the murderer is waiting at the door to give himself up. And you'd be surprised how often that happens. If people didn't confess to their crimes, the conviction rate would be far lower than it is.'

But the colonel was clearly in no mood to pursue this particular conversational gambit.

'What's the name of the officer in charge of the case?' he asked. 'I shall want to get in touch with him.'

'It's Detective Chief Inspector Sweet, sir,' Fox replied after consulting his pocketbook again. 'He'll probably ask you to identify your son's body. Not a very pleasant thing, but an evidential requirement of the law, as one might say.'

'I understand.'

'You mentioned other sons ... I don't know whether Chief Inspector Sweet has already been in touch with them ... Is it more than one, sir?'

'No. As far as I know, my other son's in London, but we don't keep in touch with one another. I can't tell you his address.' Aware that Fox was looking at him with an expression of patient expectation, he added, 'My younger son is what you call a drop-out. I've wiped my hands of him.'

'I'm sorry to hear that, sir. A lot of young folk with decent backgrounds seem to go off the rails these days and cause trouble to their parents.' He shook his head in sad reflection. 'Did he keep in touch with his older brother?'

'I believe so.'

'Perhaps he was able to help where you couldn't. There wouldn't have been the same age-gap problem.' Still mentally tut-tutting he rose to take his leave.

Poor old boy, he reflected as he drove off in his panda car. From all accounts, it should have been the younger boy who got the chop.

CHAPTER 15

Detective Chief Inspector Sweet and Detective Sergeant Adderly sat in Sweet's office in an atmosphere of cigarette smoke and gloom, the smoke being provided by Adderly and the gloom by Sweet.

Twelve days had passed since Philip Arne's death and an arrest seemed no nearer. Indeed, Sweet was sure the prospect had receded. It always was so if the first twenty-four hours passed without any clue as to who one was looking for.

He felt particularly frustrated as he had expected to have it all sewn up quite quickly. It hadn't given the appearance of becoming a baffling investigation and yet that was precisely what it had become.

'It was obviously somebody who knew him,' Adderly said, lighting a fresh cigarette from the stub of another. 'That much is certain. We can definitely rule out a casual intruder,' he went on, as though that brought them to the threshold of an exciting new discovery.

'If we're to believe the brother, it was somebody the deceased was expecting.'

'If,' Adderly said in a weighty tone. 'I don't think I'm prepared to believe very much that young man tells me. He could easily have invented that in order to conceal the fact he returned later himself and killed his brother.'

'He has an alibi of sorts.'

'One with holes the size of Dutch cheeses. Who's to say he didn't go back to his brother's flat during one of those periods when he was supposedly walking the streets of London? If only we could prove a motive.'

'It's the absence of any motive that really has us stymied,'

Sweet observed wearily. 'If only we could get a line on the girl who answered the phone when Rosa Epton called. Dammit, she must have been standing there beside the body. What the hell was she up to?'

'And how did she get in?'

'That, too.'

'Assuming she'd not been there the whole night, she must have had a key.'

'Or been admitted by the murderer.'

'The murderer isn't likely to have hung around.'

'I'm still convinced somebody went over that flat with a fine tooth comb,' Sweet remarked. 'Every clue was removed and who'd have done that but the murderer?'

'Even so, it wouldn't have taken him all night. I can't see him still there at eight the next morning to let in the girl, whoever she was.'

'I wonder why she answered the phone at all,' Sweet said in a ruminative tone.

'Unless she was expecting someone to call her there.'

'Just what I had in mind. But where does that take us? One thing for certain, Shiv Kapur knows more than he's admitting.'

Adderly nodded. 'Haven't trusted him from the outset. If you ask me, sir, it's significant that his girl-friend has disappeared. I'm sure he's spirited her out of the way, because he doesn't want us to question her. We have good information that she'd been living with him right up to the day of the murder and then suddenly she's not there any more. Gone abroad for a week or two, he says, to visit her mother in Rome.'

'It's possible that's where she is.'

'If she is in Rome, I bet he despatched her there to keep her out of our way.'

'Supposing he *doesn't* want us to interview her, does that make him a murderer?'

'We've got to establish a motive,' Adderly said vehemently. 'We shan't get anywhere until we have.'

'We can agree on that all right,' Sweet remarked drily. He rummaged through the papers littering his desk, eventually extracting the pathologist's report. 'Four separate and distinct fractures of the skull,' he read out.

'Each capable of causing death and each caused by the same sharp point of the statue's base, which had congealed blood, brain tissue and tiny splinters of bone adhering to it.' He let the report slip from his fingers. 'But not a single identifiable fingerprint on the murder weapon. That means the murderer took time afterwards to wipe it clean; and not only Lakshmi but everything else he touched . . .'

'He may have been wearing gloves,' Adderly broke in.

Sweet shook his head. 'This wasn't a premeditated murder in the sense that the murderer went equipped for the job. It was a savage, frenzied attack in the course of a violent row and afterwards he removed all traces of his presence.'

'Surely he must have got blood on his clothing?'

'I imagine he's long since destroyed anything he couldn't clean.' He glanced up at his sergeant and said sardonically, 'So all we have to do is find out the cause of the quarrel and we have the identity of the murderer.'

'Q.E.D.,' Adderly murmured.

'What's that mean?'

'*Quod erat demonstrandum.* One used to put it at the end of deductive mathematical problems at school. It means, what was to be proved.'

Sweet let out a grunt, which was his usual form of acknowledgement of Sergeant Adderly's displays of erudition. After a pause he said, 'I think I might have a day at the seaside and go and talk to Colonel Arne. I didn't have a chance to exchange more than a couple of words with him when he came to identify his son's body.'

'What do you hope to learn from him, sir?'

'I've no idea. I'd just like to probe the family background a bit. He may come up with something, but even if he doesn't, we're no worse off than at present.'

'Can't say I took to him,' Adderly observed. 'He was about as warm as a glacier and he obviously had little time for his sons.'

'That doesn't mean he mayn't be in possession of information which could help.'

'When do you propose to go, sir?'

'Probably tomorrow.'

'Like me to come with you?' Adderly asked hopefully, not because he thought it sounded a promising idea, so much as because he suddenly realised he wouldn't mind a day out himself.

But Sweet shook his head. 'You're going to spend tomorrow at Shepherd's Bush Magistrates' Court,' he said.

'I want a full report on what happens at Francis Arne's trial. We may yet discover a link between it and his brother's murder.' He gave his sergeant a mischievous smile. 'But I'll spare you a thought as I drive through the green countryside.'

CHAPTER 16

Rosa felt guilty. She had not phoned her father for a fort-night and knew that his unspoken reproaches would come down the line when she did. The trouble was she had to be in the right mood to do so, otherwise their conversations became brittle and uncomfortable and she then felt obliged to ring again immediately to try and put things right.

The Reverend Arthur Epton had spent thirty-five years as a rector of a small Herefordshire village, for the past ten of which he had been a widower. David, Rosa's older brother, lived and worked in America so that she was left to cope with him on her own. He had never been a particularly cheerful person and was even less so after a series of illnesses which he had accepted with anything but Christian resignation.

He had been proud when his daughter qualified as a soli-citor, but despondent and doubtful when she decided to make her life in London. Moreover, it was ingrained in him that solicitors who specialised in criminal work somehow sullied their honourable profession.

Nevertheless, each showed a respect and affection toward the other in a way that made contact tolerable, and Rosa still enjoyed her occasional visits to the house in which she had grown up. The peaceful countryside relaxed her as nothing else did.

On the evening before she was due to defend Francis at Shepherd's Bush Magistrates' Court, she put through a call.

'Hello, daddy, I don't seem to have rung you for a while,' she said, mustering all her cheerfulness. 'I seem to have been awfully busy of late.'

'You always say that,' he said in his naturally mournful

voice. 'I fear you work too hard. When are you going to come down for a visit?'

'I'll try and manage a weekend at the end of next month.'

'Are you generally all right?'

'I'm fine. You know that I thrive on work.'

'I don't like you being all alone in London, Rosa.'

'I'm anything but alone.'

'Living alone, I mean.'

Rosa refrained from pointing out that he'd be even less happy if she decided to live in sin, as he would call it.

After a further exchange of news which consisted largely of his bringing her up to date on the affairs of the parish, he said suddenly, 'I read in a newspaper the other day of the murder of somebody called Arne. I don't normally read such items, but the name caught my eye and I recalled your having mentioned knowing someone of that name.'

'I'm afraid it was the person I knew, Philip Arne, who's been murdered.'

'Good gracious, my child, what on earth next? What times we live in when your friends are murdered around you. I hope you're not involved in any way?'

'Actually, I'm due to defend his younger brother in court tomorrow.'

'You mean he did it?' her father asked in a scandalised voice.

'No, no, he didn't commit the murder,' Rosa said, realising too late she had created a probably irretrievable situation. 'Philip's murderer hasn't yet been caught.'

'Terrible! Terrible!' her father went on. 'And to think my own daughter is involved in such sordid happenings!'

'I'm not involved, other than professionally,' she said sharply. 'You make it sound as if I'm wallowing in vice.'

'No, of course I didn't mean that. I just pray you'll remain unscathed by all the nastiness with which you apparently have to deal.'

'Don't worry about me, daddy! The odds are I shall comfortably survive.'

When some minutes later she rang off, she sat back with a heavy sigh. If only they could keep their conversations on a lighter level, but all too often nowadays they seemed to take a sudden dive and end up in an atmosphere of strained politeness. She was never more aware, than when talking to her father, of the problems of communication. She sometimes wished that she didn't feel such a strong sense of duty toward him.

She reached for the folder labelled *Re Francis Ame* and began to turn the pages of the documents contained in it.

Come to think of it, she hadn't been too good at communicating with him either! At least she was unlikely to experience that problem with Mr Lipstead.

CHAPTER 17

'Good morning, Detective Sergeant Adderly.'

Adderly turned to find an enigmatically smiling Shiv Kapur standing immediately behind him in the lobby of the court.

'Hello, Mr Kapur, I didn't expect to see you here,' he said in a tone that clearly invited an explanation.

'Philip would have come to give his brother moral support if he'd been alive, so I considered it my responsibility, as a dear friend, to bring my humble self along in his stead.' He paused and, thrusting his head closer to Sergeant Adderly's, said, 'Is it permitted to ask how your investigation into Philip's death is proceeding?'

'Our enquiries are continuing with every sense of urgency,' Adderly replied blandly. 'Now if you'll excuse me ...'

As he pushed his way into court, he wondered what Shiv Kapur's interest in the case really was. He certainly wasn't there solely out of ties of friendship, which implied he had a more practical reason for attending.

Adderly wished he had thought to ask the smooth bastard when his girl-friend was expected back from Rome, though he realised it would take more than that to ruffle the composure of this brown fancy man with his gold rings and chains and delicate smell of toilet water. Of course I'd feel just the same about him if he were white, he quickly reassured himself. He glanced across to where Rosa was holding a whispered conversation with the prosecuting solicitor.

Jeremy Twine, the person in question, wore a permanently harassed air, brought about by being constantly thrown into court without proper time to prepare his cases.

Take this Arne case, for example. His colleague who had been supposed to present it had shoved it on his desk just as he was about to leave the office the previous evening. Admittedly there had not been much to read, just the two statements of police witnesses, but this had done nothing to diminish his unease.

He hated sus cases, he was always nervous in front of Mr Lipstead and he knew enough about Rosa to wish she wasn't defending.

If only he had opted for a nice quiet country practice instead of joining Scotland Yard's Solicitors' Branch where life was never less than hectic and court appearances could be nerve-racking.

A brief word with P.C. Paynter on his arrival at court had done nothing to allay his anxieties. He recognised the type well. Trying to elicit their evidence always made him feel like an inexperienced jockey on a headstrong horse. He wished he had gone to the lavatory, but now there wasn't time as Mr Lipstead would be taking his seat any minute.

Instead he mopped his brow and nodded gravely in response to what Rosa was saying without really taking it in.

Mr Lipstead came on to the bench and beamed all round. He looked as if he had come straight from a nice hot bath and was obviously in his cherub's mood. For the time being, at least. Rosa got a particularly warm smile; Jeremy Twine collected a mere nod.

Francis Arne's name was called and he stepped into the dock, where he glanced around him with an air of studied indifference. The clerk read out the charge of loitering with intent to commit an arrestable offence and formally explained to him his various rights, which Rosa had already done anyway. He pleaded not guilty in a tone of apparent scorn for the whole court and everyone in it and was thereafter invited by the magistrate to sit down.

'Ready to call your first witness?' Mr Lipstead enquired pointedly.

'I thought it might be of assistance, sir, if I quickly outlined the evidence to you,' Twine replied in a hopeful gush of words.

'You've only two witnesses, have you not, and both of them police officers? Well, then, let us not waste time with openings. I'm sure Miss Epton and I are quite capable of following the evidence as it's adduced. Because this is a special hearing, with time set aside, doesn't mean we can waste it unnecessarily.'

'I call Police Constable Paynter,' Twine said, wondering all over again why he put up with so much harassment. He was only twenty-nine, but already his hair was starting to fall out and after a day in front of somebody like Mr Lipstead, he felt positively middle-aged. As he waited for Paynter to take the oath, what little confidence remained in him seemed to seep away.

P.C. Paynter intoned the words of the oath with the confident air of someone on fraternal terms with the Almighty. Then producing his notebook from his tunic pocket, he laid it on the ledge in front of him, indicating he was ready to start his recital of events, which, he clearly hoped, would conclude with the defendant being despatched to prison. He had no time for young layabouts who flouted the law and preyed on society. Moreover he felt special contempt for those who had thrown away the advantages of a decent upbringing and education. In his view even outer darkness was too good for them.

Having elicited the preliminary details, Twine invited the witness to start on the substance of his evidence, an invitation P.C. Paynter accepted as it were a patriotic call to duty.

'At seven p.m. on Wednesday, 18th March, your worship, I was on plain clothes duty with Police Constable Hexham in Kenpark Square when we observed ...'

'Just confine yourself to what you observed, officer,' Mr Lipstead cut in.

For a moment Paynter looked puzzled, before deciding to press on as if nothing had happened.

'When we observed, your worship . . .'

'When *I* observed,' Mr Lipstead said testily. 'You can only give evidence as to what you yourself observed.'

'Yes, your worship. When I observed the defendant, whom I now identify, cross the road and examine a car which was parked close to the railings on the garden side of the square.'

'What make of car was it?' Twine broke in, with the air of a bystander anxious to offer his assistance.

'A Mercedes, your worship,' Paynter said, glancing about him with a look of mild triumph.

Rosa turned to Francis with a questioning expression.

'Bloody lie,' he hissed at her.

'What do you mean when you say he examined the car?' Mr Lipstead asked.

'I saw him try and open the driver's door, your worship. Then he walked to the back of the car and touched the catch on the boot.'

'Another lie,' Francis whispered furiously into Rosa's ear. 'I never went anywhere near a Mercedes.'

'What happened next?' Twine asked in a valiant attempt to assert himself.

'He returned to the side of the road where P.C. Hexham and I were keeping him under observation. He walked along the pavement for about thirty yards, frequently stopping and looking about him. Then he crossed the road again and went up to a Rolls Royce which was parked beside the railings.' The witness glanced down at his notebook. 'The car's registration number was JM 2616 . . .'

'Is that an old registration number?' Twine asked keenly.

'Yes, as I was about to add, the car was first registered in

84

1932. I saw him try the driver's door, then he disappeared behind the car. It stood higher off the ground than a modern car, your worship, so that a person standing on its far side was completely obscured.' Mr Lipstead accepted this patient exposition with an air of suppressed impatience and the witness went on, 'At the same time I saw a figure moving toward the car from the opposite direction as if to meet the defendant. P.C. Hexham and I moved across the road where I arrested the defendant. The other man ran off, pursued by P.C. Hexham, but made good his escape. I told the defendant that I was arresting him for loitering with intent to steal from parked motor cars and he made no reply. I took from him this bunch of keys, one of which, your worship, will open the doors of a number of cars of popular make. I should add, your worship, that when I went to arrest the defendant, he put up a struggle and tried to escape so that I was obliged to restrain him.'

'Thank you, officer,' Twine said with a sigh of relief and sat down.

'Yes, Miss Epton,' Mr Lipstead said encouragingly. 'I expect you wish to cross-examine.'

Rosa stood up and faced the witness with a stern expression.

'You speak of restraining the defendant, but the truth is that you gratuitously assaulted him, did you not?'

'Certainly not.'

'Didn't you twist his arm behind his back?'

'I only used such force as was reasonable,' Paynter replied.

'Reasonable for what purpose?'

'To restrain him.'

'When you effected his arrest, you took him completely by surprise, did you not?'

'Yes,' the witness said in a tone of satisfied recollection.

'So that there was never any question of his being able to escape?'

85

'His companion did.'

'I'm asking you about the defendant.'

'He might have tried to.'

'But did he?'

'He didn't have an opportunity.'

'Precisely. So why was it necessary to twist his arm behind his back and hold it in that position for over five minutes?'

'I wasn't running any risks.'

'You applied preventive force?'

'You could put it that way.'

'So there was no question of having to restrain him?'

'In my view, there was.'

'You're considerably bigger than he is, aren't you?'

'Yes.'

'I suggest that it wasn't necessary to use any force at all and that he made no effort to escape?'

'I wasn't taking any chances.'

'Is that the principle on which you work?'

'I don't know what you mean,' the witness said with a frown.

'Put the physical boot in first and ask questions afterwards.'

'Certainly not.'

Rosa put up her hands to brush back her hair which had fallen forward on either side of her face, as Mr Lipstead let out an imperceptible sigh.

'I want to ask you about this Mercedes which you say the defendant tampered with,' she went on. 'What was its registration number?'

'I can't tell you,' Paynter said with an annoyed frown.

'You mean you never made a note of it?' Rosa said in a forensically shocked tone.

'I didn't have an opportunity.'

'Perhaps your colleague will be able to tell us,' Rosa remarked, knowing full well that he wouldn't.

'Our main objective was keeping the defendant under observation and not losing sight of him. Later when I returned to the scene to obtain the number of the Mercedes, it had been moved.'

'What colour was it?'

'A dark colour.'

'Blue, red, black?'

'It was difficult to tell as the light wasn't very good at that point.'

'But good enough to enable you to see him try and open its door?'

The witness glowered. 'Yes,' he said in a tight lipped manner.

'I put it to you that he never went anywhere near a Mercedes car.'

'He did.'

'Of course, without his alleged tampering with another car, you'd have had no basis for arresting him as a suspected person when he was beside the Rolls, would you?'

'That's not for me to say.'

'It's very much for you to say,' Mr Lipstead broke in. 'Before you can arrest someone for being a suspected person loitering with intent to commit an arrestable offence, there has to have been some preceeding conduct to arouse your suspicion. As I understand your evidence, the preceding conduct was his crossing the road and trying the door of the Mercedes.'

'Yes, your worship.'

'So why did you state just now that it wasn't for you to say?'

'I didn't properly understand the question,' Paynter remarked grimly.

'Then you should have said so,' the magistrate retorted, while the witness stood bolt upright, a picture of suffused anger and indignation. 'Yes, please go on, Miss Epton,' he said turning to Rosa.

'How far were you from the defendant when, as you allege, he crossed the road to the Mercedes?'

'About forty yards.'

'Forty yards in a not very well lit square?'

'It's better lit in some places than others.'

'And what were you and P.C. Hexham pretending to do?'

'We were on plain clothes duty.'

'You've told us that, but how were you acting while you kept him under observation?'

Paynter gave a dismissive shrug. 'We were just carrying out normal duty.'

'Do you think that anyone observing you might have thought you were acting suspiciously?'

'I can't say.'

'Were you moving furtively from doorway to doorway?'

'I think P.C. Hexham stood in a doorway at one point.'

'But you generally stayed in the shadows?'

'Yes.'

'Until you crossed the road and pounced?'

'Yes.'

'The man who ran away, has he ever been traced?'

'No.'

'Have you any idea who he was?'

'No.'

'So you have no evidence that he had any connection with the defendant?'

'I had the impression that they were keeping a rendezvous beside the Rolls.'

'With a view to stealing it?' Rosa asked with an edge to her tone.

'Yes,' Paynter replied firmly, after a significant pause.

'Are you really suggesting that?'

'I am.'

'That two men arrive beside a car from opposite directions in order to steal it?'

'That was my inference'

'If that was their intention, what on earth was the defendant doing crossing the road to examine the Mercedes?'

Paynter bit his lip as he flushed angrily. 'I can't tell you, but that's what he did.'

'The key you say you found in his possession which'll open certain car doors, could it have opened the doors of either the Mercedes or the Rolls?'

'Not the Rolls.'

'What about the Mercedes?'

'I've already explained, that car had been moved by the time I returned to the scene.'

'Have you tried to trace it?'

'No.'

'Why not?'

'It didn't seem sufficiently important.'

Rosa raised a sardonic eyebrow. 'Have you thought it worthwhile to enquire at a Mercedes dealer whether that key could open the doors of any of their cars?'

'No.'

'Anyway, it was obviously useless for opening the Rolls, which, according to your evidence, was their objective. That's right, isn't it?'

'It was a key which would open a lot of car doors and I regarded that as significant.'

'Is that why you planted it on him?'

P.C. Paynter stared at Rosa as if she had suddenly stuck out a forked tongue at him.

'Would you mind repeating that?' he said, gripping the sides of the witness box until Rosa felt she could almost feel the wood splintering.

'I'm putting it to you that you planted that particular key on the ring you took from the defendant.'

'It's an outrageous suggestion.'

'So you deny it?' Rosa said mildly.

'I most certainly do.'

'You see, the defendant will say that the key is not his and was never on his ring.'

'I swear that I found that key on the ring which I took from him,' the witness said in a resounding voice.

'You've taken an oath to tell the truth, so there's no need for histrionics,' Mr Lipstead remarked sternly.

'I'm sorry, your worship, but I was upset by such a wicked suggestion.'

In making it, Rosa had been doing no more than her duty, namely to put her client's case in cross examination. Though she had small doubt that P.C. Paynter had lied about finding the key, she was still wholly in the dark as to what Francis *had* been up to in Kenpark Square that night. She was satisfied that it had not been to steal a vintage Rolls Royce. Or even to admire the beauty of its ancient lines. So what had drawn him across the road and into the shadows on its blind side? It seemed to be one of those cases where the truth also lurked in the shadows.

'Any more questions, Miss Epton?' Mr Lipstead said, breaking in on her thoughts.

'Just one further matter, sir,' she said. Turning back to P.C. Paynter, who was looking at her with suppressed venom, she went on, 'Did you test the Rolls Royce for fingerprints?'

'No, it would have been pointless. It began to rain heavily soon after I'd arrested the defendant.'

'But you didn't even try?'

'As I've explained ...'

'So there's no independent evidence that the defendant ever touched the car? We have only your word.'

'With respect, sir,' Twine broke in anxiously, 'it's not usual in such cases to call in fingerprint evidence. One has to rely on the evidence of police officers as to what happened.'

'Yes, is that all, Mr Twine?' the magistrate asked in a frosty tone.

The prosecuting solicitor sat down again quickly rather like a rabbit bolting for the safety of its burrow.

'Very well, call your next witness,' Mr Lipstead said, bringing him reluctantly back to his feet.

'Police Constable Hexham,' Twine announced with a resigned sigh.

Hexham took the oath and faced the prosecuting solicitor with an air of nervous diffidence that seemed to be reciprocated. His discomfort was increased by the implacable gaze of P.C. Paynter, who, having given his evidence, was now sitting at the back of the court.

'On 18th March this year were you on plain clothes duty with P.C. Paynter in Kenpark Square?'

'I was, your worship.'

'What time was that?'

As the witness glanced down at his notebook, Mr Lipstead broke in testily, 'Surely you can remember that, officer, without reference to your pocketbook?'

Hexham stared as if he had received a sudden stinging flesh wound in his backside.

'Yes, your worship,' he said with a gulp. 'It was seven p.m.'

'And what happened?' Twine asked.

'We saw the defendant . . .'

'You mean you saw him,' the magistrate remarked tartly.

'Yes, your worship.'

'What was he doing?'

'Acting suspiciously.'

'In what way?'

'He was examining a car parked against the railings which surround the garden in the centre of the square.'

'What make of car was it?'

Hexham glanced nervously at his notebook. 'It was a Mercedes.'

'When had you first noticed the defendant?' Mr Lipstead broke in.

'When he was crossing the road toward the car, your worship.'

'You'd not noticed him before then?' the magistrate went on with a frown.

Hexham stared helplessly at his notebook.

'No, your worship.'

'Very well, go on.'

'He tried to open one of the car doors.'

'Which?'

'The driver's door.'

Twine let out a silent sigh of relief. He didn't know which was worse, a headstrong witness like Paynter or one whose nervousness he felt to be dangerously contagious.

'What happened next?'

'He returned to the side of the road where P.C. Paynter and I were maintaining observation.'

'Did he touch any part of the Mercedes apart from the driver's door?' Twine asked like a horse making a sudden dash at a fence.

'I object to that question, sir,' Rosa said, coming to her feet. 'The witness said quite clearly that, after touching the driver's door, the defendant recrossed the road.'

Mr Lipstead nodded in a judicial manner. 'I agree, Miss Epton.' Turning his attention to the hapless witness he said severely, 'Did you see the defendant approach the back of the Mercedes?'

'I think so, your worship.'

'What do you mean, you think so?'

'He definitely did, your worship. I forgot to mention it.'

'And what did he do at the rear of the car?'

'Nothing. He just walked round the back and recrossed the road.'

'You didn't see him do anything to the rear of the car?'

Mr Lipstead went on relentlessly.

'He was hidden from my view at that point, your worship,' Hexham said miserably, aware of P.C. Paynter's scorching look on his right flank.

'What did he do after he'd returned to your side of the road?' Twine hurried on.

'He walked along the pavement for about thirty yards and then went back across the road to where the Rolls Royce was parked. Registration number JM 2616,' the witness added with an unexpected flash of confidence.

'Just one moment, officer,' Twine said anxiously. 'What was his manner as he walked along the pavement?'

'Suspicious, your worship.'

'In what way suspicious?'

'He was glancing around as if looking for someone.'

'Or something?' Mr Lipstead said. When the witness looked at him uncomprehendingly, he added, 'Why couldn't he have been looking for something as much as for someone? All you're able to say is that he was looking about him.'

'Yes, your worship.' Hexham replied stoically.

'I saw him try and open the driver's door. Then he disappeared on the far side of the car and P.C. Paynter and I decided to go and speak to him. As we crossed the road, I saw another youth close to the rear of the Rolls Royce. As I approached, he suddenly ran off. I gave chase but lost him in one of the streets leading off the square. I then returned to where P.C. Paynter had arrested the defendant. We then took him to the station where he was formally charged and cautioned. In answer to the charge, he said "It's another police frame up".'

'Did you see P.C. Paynter take possession of any keys from the defendant?'

'Yes.'

'Do you identify that bunch as the keys in question?'

'I do.'

Twine sat down and mopped his brow as Mr Lipstead gave Rosa a look of almost eager anticipation.

'Including that key which is said to open car doors?' Rosa enquired with her head cocked quizzically on one side.

'I didn't personally examine the individual keys on the ring,' the witness said in his most unhappy tone.

'So you can't really identify them, can you?'

'It looks like the same bunch.'

'Give or take a key?' Rosa remarked sardonically.

P.C. Hexham said nothing and she decided that she had made her point rather better than she had expected. It struck her that the witness wished to put as much distance as he could between himself and what had happened and that, therefore, a soft and sympathetic approach would be best.

'Are you quite sure the defendant examined a Mercedes car?' she said in a coaxing tone.

P.C. Hexham squirmed slightly. 'That's what we observed,' he said.

'We? Do you mean that's what P.C. Paynter told you he'd observed and you've adopted his evidence?'

He shook his head violently. 'No. Definitely not.'

'Why didn't either of you take the registration number of the Mercedes?'

'We didn't have an opportunity and later it had been moved. Also it was sandwiched between two other cars and one couldn't see its plates without going right up to it.'

'Have you just thought of that?'

'No . . . no.'

'P.C. Paynter never mentioned that in his evidence,' Rosa remarked, letting the implication float toward the witness like a feather in a gentle breeze.

'It was like I've said,' he replied with the air of someone resigned to a never-ending ordeal.

'As far as you could tell, did the defendant ever become

94

aware that he was being kept under observation?'

'No. He never looked in our direction at all.'

'That would be consistent with his being in the square for an entirely innocent purpose, wouldn't it?'

'I can't say.'

'Where exactly was the other youth when you first saw him?'

'He was at the rear of the Rolls Royce.'

'You hadn't seen him approaching?'

'No. He must have been moving under cover of the cars parked against the railings.'

'That's your assumption.'

'Yes.'

'How close did he come to the defendant?'

Hexham passed his tongue over his lips. 'I can't say as I couldn't quite see where the defendant was at that moment. He was somewhere behind the car.'

Mr Lipstead, who had been frowning for a while, now interrupted.

'Was it your impression, officer, that the defendant and this other person were about to keep a rendezvous on the blind side of the car; that is, between the car and the railings?'

'It could have been so, your worship.'

'If so, would they have been reasonably out of sight of anyone on the pavement side of the square?'

'That is so, your worship.'

'Hmm, I see. I'm sorry to have interrupted you, Miss Epton, please continue your cross-examination.'

'Did you put out a description of the youth you chased?'

Hexham gave an unhappy shake of the head. 'We didn't have enough to go on.'

'He took to his heels very quickly?'

'Yes.'

'Almost as if he were ready for trouble?'

'In a way, yes.'

'Far more quickly, in fact, than if he'd been an innocent pedestrian?'

'Yes.'

'How long would he and the pedestrian have been together behind the car before you and P.C. Paynter pounced?'

'Not very long.'

'Try and give me an estimate.'

'About half a minute, perhaps.'

'During which time they were out of your sight?'

Hexham nodded doubtfully as if sniffing a trap.

'Thank you. That's all I want to ask you,' Rosa said, to his obvious surprise and relief.

She turned to speak to Francis who had been making muffled sounds of scorn and frustration from time to time during the evidence of both officers.

'Just remember what I've told you when you get into the box,' she whispered. 'Just answer the questions quietly and don't try and score smart points.'

He made a rueful face. 'I'll try,' he said.

Before the hearing had began, Rosa had noticed the faithful Perry squashed against a wall at the end of a row, managing to look like the dormouse in *Alice in Wonderland*. He now gave her a wistful smile as she caught his eye.

'Well now, Miss Epton,' Mr Lipstead said in a tone which was both benign and brisk, 'I take it you're going to call your client to give the court his version of events on the evening in question.'

'Yes, sir,' Rosa replied, adding on the spur of the moment and more out of bravura than hope, 'assuming, that is, you consider he has a case to answer.'

Mr Lipstead gazed at her over the top of his spectacles like a fond uncle beaming approval at a favourite niece. Or, as the jailer reflected, a dirty old man visually undressing a pretty girl.

'Yes, Miss Epton, I think I do need to hear his evidence before reaching a verdict.' Leaning forward in his seat, he added in a rather more judicial tone, 'I am unable to rule that he has *no* case to answer.'

Invited to take the oath, Francis did so with the studied absence of conviction exhibited by most witnesses, save for police officers who are invariably at pains to show that they and the Almighty are on the same side. Watched by an attentive, bright-eyed Perry at one end of a row and an equally attentive, but wholly impassive Shiv Kapur at the other, he laid down the Testament and cast a quick nervous glance about him before focussing his gaze on Rosa.

In answer to her preliminary questions, he admitted to being Francis Richard Arne and to be living at 26 Lebon Street, W14 and, with a touch of defiance, to having no job.

'For what purpose did you go to Kenpark Square on the evening of 18th March?' Rosa asked.

'I was just out for a walk,' he replied in the offhand tone Rosa had urged him not to adopt. As if suddenly remembering this, he added, 'I often go for evening walks on my own.'

'Any particular reason for heading that way?'

'None. I was just following my nose and found myself in the square.'

'And what happened when you reached Kenpark Square?'

'I saw a vintage Rolls parked on the other side of the road and went to look at it.'

'Why?'

'Because I've always been interested in old cars.'

'Had you crossed the road earlier to look at another car?'

'No.'

'You heard the police evidence . . .'

'It's not true. I never went to look at any Mercedes. Even if I'd noticed it, which I didn't, it wouldn't even have drawn me to the edge of the pavement.'

'So you never crossed the road until you were opposite the Rolls Royce?'

'Correct.'

'When you reached the Rolls Royce, what did you do?'

'I peered through the driver's window to see the lay-out of the instrument panel.'

'That means you were on the railings side of the car?'

'Yes.'

'Did you touch the car?'

'I may have brushed against it as I leaned forward.'

'Did you try and open the driver's door?'

'Never. And if I had, I couldn't have been seen from the other side of the road.'

'Did you go to the back of the car?'

'No.'

'Had you been aware of being kept under observation?'

'I'd noticed two men some distance behind me on the pavement, but I didn't pay them any attention.'

'Did you know the other man who approached the Rolls and later ran away?'

'No. I'd never seen him before.'

'You weren't meeting him there by arrangement?'

'Definitely not. Why should I want to meet anyone in a place like that?'

'Did you exchange any words with him?'

'I think he said something like, "she's a beauty, isn't she?" That was the first I knew he was there.'

'What happened after that?'

'I was suddenly seized and my arm was wrenched behind my back.'

'It's alleged that you tried to resist arrest, is that true?'

Francis made a derisive noise. 'Even if I'd wanted to, I didn't have a chance. He nearly broke my arm.'

'I want you to look at this bunch of keys, are they yours?'

'All except one are mine. The one that's supposed to open cars doors doesn't belong to me.'

'How did it get on the ring?'

'You'd better ask P.C. Paynter.'

'You're saying it was planted on you?'

'It must have been.'

Rosa glanced quickly through her notes; then pushing her hair back from her face, she fixed Francis with a serious look and said, 'Did you have any intention of stealing cars or stealing from them when you went to Kenpark Square that evening?'

'I did not. It's an absurd suggestion. What would I do with a vintage Rolls when I can't even afford a bicycle? And as for stealing from it, as far as I'm aware there was nothing there to steal.'

Mr Lipstead looked sharply at Jeremy Twine. 'You didn't adduce any evidence of larcenable property inside the car, did you, Mr Twine?'

'No, sir. Perhaps I could clear the point up with the officer, if you'll . . .'

'It's too late now to rectify the omission – even assuming it's capable of remedy.' He switched his attention back to Rosa. 'Any further questions, Miss Epton?'

But Rosa felt that the examination-in-chief of her client had finished on an upward note and it was the right moment to resume her seat.

Twine rose to cross-examine with all the enthusiasm of a boxer longing only for the final bell. Francis watched him warily.

'Are you seriously suggesting that the police have invented seeing you cross the road to examine the Mercedes?' he asked in a voice that sought to convey the wild absurdity of such an idea.

'All I know is that I didn't,' Francis replied evenly.

It was the right answer in the right tone Rosa noted with satisfaction.

'So you're accusing them of lying under oath?' Twine

went on, as if drawn mechanically toward a chasm.

'I'm not making any accusations. I'm just saying that I did not cross the road and look at any Mercedes.'

Once more Rosa silently applauded the answer and the manner in which it was given. It seemed, after all, as if he had heeded her advice on how to conduct himself in the witness box.

'But are you seriously suggesting that the police have made up that part of their evidence?' Twine said desperately.

'Do you really wish to go on pursuing that point?' Mr Lipstead enquired with a note of exasperation. 'There's a clear conflict of evidence which you're not going to resolve in cross-examination.'

It struck Rosa as a slightly unfair, even dangerous, intervention. On the other hand, if the magistrate had already made up his mind on the particular point, he may have wished to head the prosecuting solicitor off before he dug too deep a grave for his two police witnesses.

Certainly his cross-examination had done nothing so far to enhance their credibility.

He glanced hastily down at his notebook before raising his head and fixing Francis with a look of frowning intensity.

'But you admit that you crossed the road to go and look at the Rolls Royce?' he said, as if delivering a small coup de grace.

'Yes.'

'Do you often examine cars in the dark?'

'If they're sufficiently old and interesting.'

'Even though you can't see them properly?'

'I could see well enough for my purpose.'

'And what was your purpose?'

Mr Lipstead sighed heavily. 'He's already told us that several times over,' he remarked with asperity. 'He's interested in vintage cars.'

'I put it to you,' Twine went on, stung by the intervention, 'that your real purpose was to see what you could steal from it. Isn't that right?'

'No.'

'Then why did you try and open the driver's door?'

'I didn't.'

'So once more the police are lying, is that what you're saying?'

'All I'm saying is that I never tried to open any of its doors.'

'Do you really expect the court to believe that?'

Mr Lipstead squirmed impatiently and Rosa kept her feelings masked. Everyone knew that cross-examination was not an easy art, but the unfortunate Jeremy Twine seemed particularly inept as one ill-conceived question followed another.

'I hope so,' Francis replied, with something like a wisp of a smile.

'I put it to you that you were up to no good when you crossed over to the Rolls Royce?'

'And what's that supposed to mean?' Mr Lipstead enquired.

'That his motive was dishonest, sir,' Twine retorted crossly.

'I see. Well, go on.'

'Isn't it also right that you've lied in the witness box in order to save your skin?'

'No.'

'And isn't it also right that you've been prepared to cast wicked slurs on the veracity of two young police constables?'

To this the witness responded with a helpless shrug and Jeremy Twine quickly sat down, wiping a hand across his glistening forehead.

Rosa had never shown the tendency of many advocates

to enjoy the sound of their own voices. Moreover, she never believed in wasting time by knocking on open doors and in the present case she felt reasonably confident that the magistrate was minded to acquit her client.

In these circumstances she addressed him for a mere three and a half minutes, referring briskly to the inconsistencies revealed in the prosecution's evidence and to the defendant's persistent denial of any wrongdoing. She deftly reminded Mr Lipstead of the salient features which pointed not so much to her client's innocence as to the failure of the prosecution to prove its case beyond reasonable doubt.

When she sat down, Mr Lipstead thanked her for her help and, placing the tips of fingers delicately together, said, 'I am not satisfied that the prosecution has discharged its onus of proof in this case and I therefore dismiss the charge.' In a more ominous tone, he added, 'In all the circumstances, I think the less I say the better.' He gave Jeremy Twine a nod and turning to Rosa went on, 'Once again, Miss Epton, this court is indebted to you for your assistance in a worrying case.'

Rosa bowed her acknowledgement of the bouquet, but blushed when she intercepted the jailer's sardonic gaze.

Francis, who seemed unmoved by his acquittal, did nevertheless thank her for her efforts, while Perry stood by wreathed in happiness.

She was gathering up her papers when a voice behind spoke to her.

'You won't remember me, Miss Epton, but I'm Shiv Kapur. We met once at one of Philip's parties and he often spoke about you. If I may be permitted to say so, Francis was an extremely fortunate young man in having your services. I know how grateful Philip would have been.' He paused, fixing Rosa with a long, unfathomable look which she found quite mesmerising. 'Philip's death is a great tragedy to all his friends. We can only hope that it will not go unavenged for much longer.' He lowered his eyes and moved back a fraction. 'I trust we shall meet again soon, Miss Epton. Meanwhile, let me repeat my congratulations on your fine performance on behalf of Francis. Rest assured that I shall keep the brotherly eye on him Philip would have wished.' He gave a quick glance about him. 'I will have a word with him now before I leave. Perhaps he would like a lift in my car.' Giving Rosa a brilliant smile, he hurried after Francis who was just disappearing through the door with the faithful Perry immediately behind him.

As Rosa packed her papers into her document case, she wondered what had motivated Shiv Kapur's flowery approach. She couldn't believe it was purely an act of courtesy.

CHAPTER 18

Detective Chief Inspector Tom Sweet arrived in Worthing about eleven o'clock and called in at the local police station to introduce himself to the officer with whom he had spoken on the telephone.

When the latter explained the various exigencies that had arisen that day which made it difficult to find an officer to accompany him to Colonel Arne's and asked apologetically if he would mind foregoing the usual courtesy, Sweet was secretly relieved and able to reply with complete honesty that he quite understood.

For the next few minutes they discussed the case, in the course of which Sweet said gloomily that he feared his enquiry was in danger of running into the ground and that he had not come to Worthing with any great hope of learning much from the deceased's father. It was, as he put it, a question of having reached the stage of looking under even unpromising stones.

Shortly afterwards he set off with directions on how to reach the colonel's house, which was set a quarter of a mile back from the seafront in an area of middle-class prosperity.

Colonel Arne himself opened the front door and gave Sweet a tight-lipped welcome, his clipped moustache bristling with suspicion.

'Detective Chief Inspector Sweet, is it?' he remarked and, without waiting for an answer, led the way inside.

They went into the drawing-room where he motioned Sweet to a chair, before going and standing with his back to the fireplace.

'I gather you've come to see me about my dead son?'

'Yes.' Sweet sighed. 'The truth is that the enquiry is proving more difficult than I'd expected.'

'In what way, difficult?'

'An absence of leads. I confess I never expected it to be as difficult to solve, but we seem to run into nothing but dead ends. And yet I still feel that the solution is only just out of sight.'

'You've not found an obvious suspect?'

'No. But more importantly we've not discovered a motive.'

Colonel Arne frowned at the wall while he digested this.

'Might it have been a casual intruder?' he asked turning his cold grey gaze back on Sweet.

'The one thing of which I am certain is that the murderer was known to your son.'

'He certainly mixed with a strange crowd.'

'Do you have any theories yourself, sir, as to who and why?'

'None. As you're probably aware, we weren't on very close terms. In my view, he was wasting his life and he knew of my disapproval.'

'Working for a charitable trust isn't necessarily wasting one's life.' But Colonel Arne merely compressed his lips into a forbidding line and said nothing 'What about your son, Francis?' Sweet went on.

'I can't tell you anything about him, as he's completely out of my life.'

'Did you know that he's appearing in court today?'

Colonel Arne looked at him sharply.

'No, what's he done now?'

'He's charged with being a suspected person loitering with intent. I gather he was arrested trying to open car doors.'

'Oh! Well, I didn't know.'

'He's being defended by a solicitor who was a friend of your elder son. A woman named Rosa Epton.'

'Never heard of her.'

105

'It was Philip who asked her to take the case on.'

'What are you trying to tell me, chief inspector?'

Sweet shook his head. 'I just wondered whether you knew any of this.'

'I've already told you, no.'

'There seems to have been a certain brotherly bond between your two sons,' Sweet remarked, though without much hope of coaxing anything useful out of this iron figure, who stood observing him with chilly disfavour.

'So I believe.' After a pause in which he seemed to be wrestling with a decision whether to say anything further, he went on, 'My sons have brought us endless trouble, particularly the younger, and I can never forgive them the grief and distress they caused my poor wife. For her sake, I always sought to avoid an open breach and succeeded to some extent so far as Philip was concerned. Now, he is dead and I have no wish to be reminded of either of them. If that sounds harsh, I can only say that you and others might feel the same if you'd been through what we have in the way of disappointment and let-down.'

Sweet was taken aback by the bitterness of his words. His chief thought was that he was confronted by someone of remarkable unforgivingness. Moreover, that his sons must have inherited their characters from somewhere. There had obviously been an utter failure of communication between father and sons, but whose fault had that been, he wondered? He also couldn't help wondering what different light Mrs Arne might have been able to shed on the embittered relationship, had she still been alive.

After he had finished speaking, Colonel Arne stared sternly at the wall on the other side of the room, his mouth puckered in an expression of disdain.

Sweet's gaze shifted to a small dark oval patch on the wall to the left of the fireplace. Something had hung there until recently, leaving the surrounding area to fade. Colonel Arne seemed to intercept his gaze, for he suddenly, and with studied casualness, shifted slightly so that the patch became hidden from Sweet's view.

At first Sweet thought it must be his own naturally suspicious mind that made him believe it had been a deliberate shift of stance, for why should anyone want to hide a harmless patch on the wall? And yet he felt certain that the tiny movement had been deliberate.

Colonel Arne now cleared his throat.

'I'm afraid my younger son started to go off the rails while he was still at school,' he said with an abruptness that caused Sweet to blink. 'He was expelled for being in possession of marijuana. That was the beginning of his downward path.'

'A lot of people experiment with pot these days,' Sweet said reasonably. 'It's often no more than a phase of growing up.'

'I'm sorry to hear a senior police officer condoning the use of drugs,' the colonel said glacially.

Tom Sweet decided that it would be better not to comment, but the longer he remained in Colonel Arne's company, the less sympathy he felt toward him. It wasn't that he would ever have found him congenial, but a man who had not long ago lost his wife and more recently still had a son brutally murdered, not to mention another adrift in a fringe life of crime, would normally have stirred his sense of compassion. As it was, however, all his natural springs of human feeling were suddenly dry.

Perhaps father and son had deserved each other, he reflected as he got up to leave.

Colonel Arne accompanied him to the front door.

'I'm afraid you've had a rather wasted journey,' he remarked, as he held it open.

'There's nothing unusual about that in a police enquiry,' Sweet replied equably.

He had a distinct feeling that the colonel had been trailing his coat when he made this observation, but Chief Inspector Sweet had no intention of assuaging his curiosity.

CHAPTER 19

It was mid-afternoon before Sweet arrived back in London to find Sergeant Adderly in a state of bubbling impatience.

He had felt in no mood to hurry back and, on leaving Colonel Arne, had driven down to the sea front where he had parked his car and gone for a walk along the beach, trudging over the shingle to the water's edge. There he had spent several minutes searching for flat stones with which to play ducks and drakes. With one stone, he achieved six hops and felt childishly pleased with himself. He would like to have lingered longer, but, short-lived as it was, his truancy left him with an uplifted spirit which is more than an immediate return to London would have done.

'Learn anything, sir?' Adderly loyally enquired as he came bustling in before Sweet had had time to sit down.

It was apparent, however, that his need was to talk much more than to listen and Sweet, who was still mentally sorting out his impressions of his visit to Colonel Arne, was ready to oblige.

'How did the case go this morning?' he asked, delivering the hoped-for-cue.

'Arne was acquitted,' Adderly said in a grim voice. 'What's more, I shall be very surprised if a complaint isn't lodged against the two officers. It was an embarrassing cock-up from start to finish, not made any less so by the chap they sent along to prosecute, who was guaranteed to make things even worse.'

'What sort of complaint are you talking about?'

'Oh, for just a few peccadillos like assault and perjury and attempting to pervert the course of justice. It was obvious, to me at any rate, that it was a trumped-up charge.'

'To the magistrate, too, I gather.'

'He spared our blushes too by saying the minimum when he threw the case out.'

'I don't consider my blushes to be involved,' Sweet observed.

'You'd have been as embarrassed as anyone, sir, if you'd been there.'

'O.K., so Arne was acquitted, but how does that affect our enquiry?'

Sweet could tell from Adderly's expression that there was more to come. He knew from experience that his sergeant fancied himself as a narrator.

'After it was all over, I went back to the station to find out what I could about the background to this spectacular debacle.' Sweet closed his eyes for a moment and opened them to fix Adderly with a warning look. 'It seems, sir, that P.C. Paynter has been in trouble before for taking the bit between his teeth and trying to emulate Superman. At the moment there's no more than conjecture, but the inference is that Paynter learnt from an informant that there was to be a hand-over of drugs in Kenpark Square that evening. Instead of reporting the matter to his superiors he decided to mount his own little operation and bring off the coup of the century. I gather it's typical of him, though he probably won't have many more opportunities of going bust for glory. Anyway, things went wrong – I don't know what else he expected – the man with whom Arne is supposed to have had a rendezvous made his escape and hasn't been seen since, and Arne was arrested without a sniff of any drug on his person. So our bright young constable is left to think up something pretty quickly. Hence the charge under Section 4, Vagrancy Act and the allegation that he'd been observed tampering with parked cars.' He paused and blew out his cheeks to make a derisory sound. 'That's about the long and short of the sorry story. Needless to say there's going to be an internal enquiry whether or not any official complaint is made by Miss Epton on behalf of her client. Incidentally, I'd not heard her in court. She's not bad. In fact she was extremely effective.'

Sweet gave an abstracted nod. 'If this was a drugs hand-over, which way was the stuff going?'

'Who knows? As I said, sir, it's all conjecture at the moment because Paynter's not the sort of person to kneel on the mat and say, "Sorry, folks, I made a balls-up, but I promise not to do it again." He'll brazen it out for as long as he can. The other officer, Hexham, is much more likely to break. My guess is that he was dragged into it against his will.'

'If Arne was the hander-over where'd he get the stuff from?' Sweet said in a thoughtful voice.

'Just what I've been wondering, sir,' Adderly remarked.

'And what sort of quantity are we talking about? What type of drug for that matter?'

'I don't imagine it was just a few limp shreds of pot.'

'If it was hard stuff, there could have been big money involved. Supposing Arne was there to receive it, what was he proposing to do with it? And where'd he get the money to buy the stuff?'

'As to all that, sir, you may be interested to know that Shiv Kapur was in court and drove Arne away afterwards.'

'Interesting, indeed,' Sweet remarked. 'Assuming this drug theory has any basis in fact, I'd be inclined to believe that Arne was the distributor rather than the recipient. By the way, how much money did he have on him when he was arrested?'

'Only a few pounds.'

'So maybe the other chap made off with the stuff without paying for it. That could have left Arne with a lot of egg on his face.'

'Not as much as P.C. Paynter is going to end up with,'

111

Adderly observed grimly.

'I'm not concerned with Paynter's face, with or without egg. I'm only interested in where these drugs came from and were going to, assuming young Master Arne was a mere link in a chain.' He was thoughtful for a moment. 'I can begin to see a possible connection between this case and Philip Arne's murder.'

CHAPTER 20

Rosa saw nothing further of Francis over the next two days. Indeed, in one sense her professional duty toward him had been discharged and she had no reason to see him again. On the other hand, she had told him to make an appointment and come into the office to discuss the question of a formal complaint against P.C.s Paynter and Hexham. Moreover, so long as Philip's murder remained unsolved, there was always the possibility of his younger brother being taken in for further interrogation.

As to the complaint aspect, Rosa was torn two ways. On the face of things, a written complaint to the Commissioner would be fully warranted and she would normally have had no hesitation in so advising. Her reservation sprang from the fact that she still didn't know what her client *had* been up to that evening. Admittedly one didn't have to be as pure as driven snow in order to make justified accusations against the police, but it was desirable to know what might be hurled back at you. It was almost axiomatic that the police counter-attacked wherever possible.

In the brief talk she had had with Francis on conclusion of the case, she had found him less vindictive than he had been before, which was one reason why she had suggested a short period for reflection before a decision was taken. She had hoped to be able to discuss the pros and cons with her partner, Robin, but he had gone up to Birmingham on a case and would be away for most of the week. It was rare for either of them to appear outside London, but he always seemed to be away when she most needed his advice. And it was not the sort of matter to canvass with him over the telephone. However, a few days wouldn't make that

113

much difference, though she held the view that if you were going to lodge a complaint of this nature, you should bang it in as soon after the event as possible.

There then occurred one of those coincidences that completely reshape events.

Three days after the case at Shepherd's Bush Magistrates' Court, she found herself in one of the East London courts. It was one in which she had never previously appeared and the case was heard by a magistrate whom she knew only by name. He was new to the bench and had not had time to develop any idiosyncrasies. He fined her client £50 for shop-lifting a packet of wine gums, a tube of tooth-paste and a plastic comb and moved briskly on to his next case.

As Rosa strolled along a sunny pavement on her way back to her car, which was parked some distance away, she took time to glance around her. It was not a very salubrious area, but she always enjoyed peering at unfamiliar shops and buildings.

Suddenly her eye was caught by a sign on a distinctly shabby door next to a sordid-looking cafe.

'Reynolds-Bailey Trust. First Floor,' it read.

The words had faded with age and the surrounding paint was peeling.

She opened the door and found herself staring up a steep flight of narrow wooden stairs. Wondering exactly what she was doing, she closed the door behind her and went up. She decided that it was curiosity to see where Philip had worked that prompted her to go and introduce herself to someone.

At the top of the stairs, a further sign indicated a door on the right which had "knock and enter" written on it.

Rosa did both and found herself in a small cheerless room which was deserted apart from an emaciated-looking cat asleep on a chair.

There was a door marked "private" on the other side of

the room and through this there suddenly appeared a girl of about Rosa's own age. She was wearing jeans and a purple sweater several sizes too large.

She gave Rosa a friendly smile.

'Can I help you?' she said. 'Not that I really work here. I'm just lending a hand as they're short-staffed.'

For several seconds Rosa just stared at her, until the girl's expression changed to a suspicious frown.

'I'm terribly sorry,' she managed to say at last.

'I suddenly felt most odd. I must have come up the stairs too quickly ... And I didn't have time for breakfast this morning ...'

The girl smiled again. 'They are a bit steep. I was about to explain that I'm the only person here at the moment, but if you care to leave a message, I'll see that someone gets it.'

'I was passing and happened to see the name on the door downstairs and thought it was an opportunity to drop in and say thank you to someone for the help the Trust gave an old aunt of mine when she became bedridden a few years ago. She's dead now,' she added quickly, hoping that her story didn't sound quite as preposterous as it did to her own ears.

The girl gave her a puzzled frown. 'I didn't know they helped anyone's ancient aunts,' she said. With a giggle she added, 'Assuming your old aunt wasn't an Indian seaman. Are you sure you've got the right place?'

'I thought I had, but obviously not. I'm terribly sorry to have troubled you.'

'Not at all. You're sure you don't want to leave any message? Mr Kapur will be back in about an hour.'

Rosa shook her head. 'How stupid can one get?' she said with a helpless shrug.

Five minutes later she was back at her car, her mind still in a turmoil, for she hadn't the slightest doubt that the girl she had just been talking to was the same one who had answered Philip's telephone.

CHAPTER 21

When Shiv Kapur arrived back at the drab office of the Reynolds-Bailey Trust, Nadia hurled herself into his arms and smothered his face in kisses.

'I think something awful's happened,' she said, bursting into tears.

Disentangling himself from her distinctly wet embrace, he said a trifle impatiently, 'What are you talking about?'

'There was a girl up here a moment ago and she behaved most oddly. She pretended she'd made a mistake and come to the wrong place, but it was only after ... after I'd begun speaking.'

'Describe her to me,' he said sharply. When she had done so, he remarked, 'That was almost certainly Rosa Epton and from what you say she obviously recognised your voice.' He took a step toward the door marked "private". 'I've got to think and think quickly.'

'You're not angry with me, are you darling?'

'Not if you do as I tell you.'

'You know I will.'

'Good.'

'Am I still your goddess?' she asked in a tone in which hope and anxiety were mixed.

'Not if you pester me with silly questions. Now sit down and don't talk while I decide what to do. Time mayn't be on our side.'

CHAPTER 22

As a result of Sergeant Adderly's report on the Arne case, Chief Inspector Sweet re-read all the statements that had been taken in the course of his murder enquiry, hoping some detail, hitherto overlooked, would draw attention to itself in the light of his fresh information. But as so often in a bogged-down enquiry, his initial flicker of hope was soon extinguished. Nevertheless, he decided it was time for Shiv Kapur to be interviewed afresh. After all, by attending Francis Arne's trial he had put himself in the frame, if only in a blurred sort of way.

It was while he was deciding on his strategy, which, in this instance, meant no more than wondering whether to wait and hear if the drug passing theory had gained greater substance or whether it still remained in the realm of conjecture, that he received a call from Rosa.

'I can tell you who answered Philip Arne's phone the morning after his death,' she said without any preliminaries. 'It was Shiv Kapur's girl-friend.'

'Nadia Beresford?' Sweet said when he had overcome his surprise at this bit of news.

'If that's her name. I'd better tell you what happened.'

When she had finished, Sweet said, 'I'm greatly obliged to you, Miss Epton. Indeed, that's an understatement; I'm indebted to you.' He paused. 'Incidentally, I hear you triumphed in court the other day. Maybe we could have an off-the-record chat about your case?'

'Maybe,' Rosa replied cautiously.

'I'd be interested to know what your client was really up to in Kenpark Square that evening.'

So would I, she felt like replying. Instead she said, 'I doubt whether my professional conscience would allow me to assist you that much, Mr Sweet.'

He laughed. 'Perhaps not, though an unofficial exchange of views wouldn't be amiss. You see, I now believe there could be a link between your case and Philip Arne's death.'

'In what way?' Her tone was wary.

'I'm afraid it's my turn to claim privilege of information. For the time being, at least.'

'I hope you'll remember that I still represent Francis Arne,' she said after a pause.

'I certainly will now that you've told me. I'd assumed that you were now *functus*. Isn't that what you lawyers call it? Anyway, he's a lucky fellow to have your services, Miss Epton.'

'So, should you decide to interrogate him further, I shall be glad if you will let me know.'

'I think that could become a distinct possibility,' Sweet remarked. 'And of course I'll let you know. Meanwhile, thank you again for the information you've just given me. This could be a real breakthrough.'

He put down the receiver and looked at his watch. Twenty minutes before one o'clock. If Shiv Kapur had spirited Nadia away once already, he could do so again, particularly if he suspected that Rosa had recognised her voice.

Ordering a car to stand by to take him to the office of the Reynolds-Bailey Trust, he put through a quick call to Detective Inspector Parrish who was stationed in that area.

'Know anything about the Reynolds-Bailey Trust on your manor, Bob?' he asked.

'Can't say I do. I can make a few enquiries if you want. Anyway, what's up?'

When Sweet arrived after a frustrating drive through the City with its midday traffic, Detective Inspector Bob Parrish was sitting in his car outside the office of the Reynolds-

Bailey Trust. He got out as Sweet's car pulled up.

'I came round immediately, Tom, but the place is all locked up. I suppose it could be that they're closed for lunch. I made a few quick enquiries before I left, but they don't seem to have come to our notice in any serious way. Apparently an Indian came along to the station a few weeks ago and complained they'd refused to help him and had thrown him out, but that seems to be about all.'

'Never any suggestion that there might be drug trafficking going on behind the scenes?'

'Not a whisper. Is that what you've heard, Tom?'

Sweet proceeded to relate what had happened. When he finished, Parrish said, 'As a matter of fact, I had a word with the sergeant who keeps an eye on our drug scene and he said that, though some of the people seen entering and leaving the premises were known drug-users in a small way, there'd never been any hint that they obtained their supplies there.' He became suddenly thoughtful. 'Mind you, it wouldn't be a bad front, would it? I wonder . . . I wonder . . .'

Sweet waited for him to go on, but Parrish fell curiously silent. After a while, he said, 'Well, Tom, are we going to hang on and see if anyone returns or shall we go away and have a pint of beer and come back later?'

'I'm all for the second, providing someone can keep a quiet eye on the place while we're gone.'

'I've got a young D.C. in my car. He can do that. Poor sod's just spent eight days keeping watch on a warehouse from which stuff was disappearing by the lorry-load, so half an hour watching the front door of the Reynolds-Bailey Trust will seem like a holiday.'

When forty minutes later they returned, it was to be told that nobody had come and nobody had left.

By three o'clock Sweet decided that he had hung around long enough. Whatever the reason, the Reynolds-Bailey Trust seemed to have closed for the day.

119

But hanging around is often part of a police investigation and he was later that day to spend further hours waiting outside a block of flats in South Kensington where Shiv Kapur lived. It was around seven o'clock that evening he let out a heartfelt sigh as he saw Kapur drive his BMW 323i down the slope which led to an underground garage.

He and Adderly immediately got out of their own car and hurried after him to find he had already parked his car and was standing by the lift.

'Good evening, Mr Kapur, I seem to have spent most of the day looking for you, but here we are met up at last. You know Detective Sergeant Adderly, of course?'

Kapur glanced impassively from one to the other, though Sweet thought he detected a sudden alerting of his senses.

'Good evening, chief inspector and to you, too, detective sergeant. I assure you that I've not been deliberately avoiding you, but I've had a particularly busy day and' – here he gave one of his dazzling smiles – 'you've obviously not been looking in the right places.' The lift arrived and they got in, Kapur pressing the button for the sixth floor. 'I hope you're not going to keep me in suspense about the purpose of your visit.'

'Shall we find Miss Beresford in your flat?' Sweet enquired, aware that, unless she had slipped into the building by a back way, she was certainly not there.

Kapur's expression clouded for a moment, as though he found the question puzzling.

'No, she is away.'

'But I understand she has come back from Rome.'

'Back from Rome, and now away again,' Kapur said with an apologetic smile.

'Where can we find her?'

The Indian shook his head sadly. 'I'm afraid I'm unable to tell you. She is staying with friends and quite forgot to leave me her telephone number.'

'Where do these friends live?'

120

'Somewhere up north. Yorkshire, I think it is.'

'When did she go?'

'Only this very afternoon,' Kapur said blandly. 'As a matter of fact she spent the morning helping out at my office in the Reynolds-Bailey Trust.'

So he knows why we're here, Sweet reflected. Adroit of him to have got that in first, the smooth so-and-so.

'I take it she'll be in touch with you?'

'I certainly hope so, but she can be a scatty girl and if she's having a good time ...' He let the sentence tail away. 'After all, it's not as if she's my wife,' he added with a tiny smile. 'Is it permitted to ask why you wish to see her with such apparent urgency?'

The lift arrived at their floor and they followed Kapur into his flat. Not until he had closed the door behind them did Sweet vouchsafe an answer.

'I suspect you know very well why I wish to see her, Mr Kapur.' The Indian gave a small helpless shrug and Sweet went on, 'I have good reason to believe that she was in Philip Arne's flat after he had been murdered and before his body was discovered. In which case, she has quite a lot of explaining to do.'

'I see.'

'Moreover, I suspect you know all this and have been deliberately keeping her out of our way.'

'Why should I do that, chief inspector?'

'Because you know much more about Arne's murder than you've told us.'

'You're accusing me of murdering my friend?' Kapur said, with a pained expression.

'Not yet, but that may come,' Sweet said in an ominous tone. 'It depends on you.'

Kapur drew a deep breath and expelled it slowly, and then repeated the excercise.

'Controlled breathing. Very important for concentrating

the mind,' he remarked. 'But please let me offer you some hospitality! Why should we stand here like three statues when we could be seated with drinks in our hands? I know that Sergeant Adderly likes pale ale, but for you, chief inspector, a glass of Chivas Regal with Malvern water and no ice. How about it?'

'I'll also have a pale ale,' Sweet said dourly.

'I shall join you in a pineapple juice. I neither drink alcohol, nor do I smoke.'

'But you enjoy the company of pretty girls,' Adderly said with a faint leer.

Kapur smiled. 'My years of chastity ended at the age of thirteen.'

'And now let's get back to the point,' Sweet growled. 'Namely, what was Miss Beresford doing in Philip Arne's flat on the morning after his murder? We know she was there and you know she was. So?'

'So, chief inspector.'

'She must have had a key. How else did she get in? Did you give her one? And, most important of all, what was she doing there? Three questions, Mr Kapur, to which I'm certain you can give me the answers.'

For a full half-minute Shiv Kapur stared into the glass of pineapple juice which he held cupped in his hands like a crystal ball, as if searching for the answer to Sweet's questions.

Eventually he looked up and said, 'You're right, chief inspector, it is time for me to tell you all I know. If I have not done so before, it is solely because I have had the interests of others at heart. I have sought to prevent the innocent from unjust suspicion. I ask you most sincerely to believe that, chief inspector.'

'It's facts I'm interested in,' Sweet remarked, reflecting that Kapur even outdid Sergeant Adderly when it came to flowery phrases.

'It's true that Nadia did go to Philip's flat that morning, and that she found him dead ...'

'Why did she go?' Sweet broke in.

'Because I requested her to. I was worried that something had happened to Philip. While she was at the flat the phone rang and it was Miss Epton. Nadia was sure it must be me or she'd never have answered. She thought I was calling to find out what had happened to Philip.'

'What made you think that anything had happened to him?'

'I was about to come to that, chief inspector. It must have been around five o'clock the previous evening when Philip called me. He said he was expecting his brother and that he was set to have an almighty row with him. I begged him not to say or do anything he might later regret, but he said he felt a showdown was unavoidable. We didn't talk for long as I was about to go out. When I got home around ten o'clock. I called Philip's number but there was no reply. I went on trying until after one without getting any answer. In view of what he had said earlier, I was filled with foreboding. Nevertheless I decided to wait until morning before taking any action. Between six and seven I tried his number several more times. I then asked Nadia if she would go to the flat and find out what had happened ...'

'Why didn't you go yourself?' Sweet enquired in a steely tone.

'I know what you're thinking, chief inspector, and you're right to think it, but I felt that Nadia was likely to attract less attention than myself and as we didn't know what to expect, it seemed best to keep a low profile. O.K., not very brave, not very meritorious, but prudent in all the circumstances.' He paused with a faraway expression before going on. 'Of course, the poor child found him lying on the floor horribly murdered and returned here in a state of utter shock. If you had not discovered the murder very soon afterwards, I swear to you, chief inspector, that I was going to report it to the police.'

'How did she get into the flat?' Sweet asked, brushing aside the Indian's protestation of good intentions.

'Philip always insisted I keep a key.'

'You told me you didn't have one,' Adderly broke in.

'I know ... I know. I'm afraid I wasn't then ready to tell you everything.'

'Why not?'

'Is that not obvious?' he asked in an anguished voice. 'The last thing I wanted was to cast suspicion on the brother of my closest friend. On someone whom I now more than ever regard as my own brother.'

'You mean Francis Arne?' Sweet said, and Kapur nodded sadly. 'Did Philip give you any idea what he and his brother were going to row about?'

Kapur let out a long, heavy sigh. 'Against all my advice, Philip had become involved in drugs. I begged him not to, but he said he needed the money ...'

'You mean drug-trafficking, not just his own use of drugs?' Sweet interrupted.

'Yes,' Kapur said in a painful whisper. 'On this particular occasion he used his brother as a courier. He only did it because Francis also needed money and had been plaguing him. Francis was supposed to hand over a packet of heroin and collect £2,000 for it. But the contact made off with the heroin without ever handing over the money.'

'This, I take it, was what was happening in Kenpark Square the evening Francis Arne was arrested.'

'Yes ... I'm filled with horror every time I think of it. Horror that Philip allowed himself to become involved in that sort of thing.'

'So the row was because Francis had bungled his part in the affair and the two brothers had lost out all round,' Sweet observed in a thoughtful voice. He glanced at Sergeant

Adderly. 'Which seems to convert conjecture into fact?'

Adderly nodded.

'So your theory, Mr Kapur, is that Francis killed his brother in the course of the almighty row that took place,' Sweet went on.

Kapur fluttered his hands and raised his eyes sorrowfully toward the ceiling. 'Please, chief inspector, am I not unhappy enough without being asked for theories? I have now told you all I know. I have made a clean breast and I ask only that you should respect my sensibilities.'

'If you have now told the truth, I'm sure it's out of self-interest,' Sweet said brutally. 'By not reporting the murder as soon as you could, you've hindered the course of justice and that's a very serious matter. You're certain to hear more about it in due course.'

'You're a hard man, chief inspector,' Kapur remarked with a sorrowful note of reproach.

'I'm a realist, Mr Kapur, which brings me to another straight question requiring a straight answer. How long did Nadia remain at the flat that morning?'

'Mere minutes! She was so shocked by what she found.'

'But surely she wasn't surprised in the light of what you've told me? After all, you suspected something awful had happened. You've said so.'

'Yes, but ...' He shook his head as if admitting defeat in his efforts to explain himself to a heartless police officer.

'Would it be fair to suggest she stayed long enough to remove any fingerprints and other incriminating evidence?' Sweet asked.

Kapur gave him a look of horror. 'You can't mean that, chief inspector?'

'Why not?'

'You're as good as accusing me of killing my friend.'

'Did you?'

'No! No!'

'I shall want to check your movements of the previous evening.'

Beads of perspiration glistened on Kapur's forehead, and on his upper lip which he wiped clean with his tongue.

'I have nothing to fear,' he said in a voice that trembled.

'That's all right then.'

When some minutes later the two officers took their leave, he seemed to have recovered some of his composure. The enigmatic smile was back in place, though the eyes showed that a frightened man lurked behind it.

'I want to know as soon as you hear from Nadia,' Sweet said at the door. 'Unless you've decided that you know where she is after all.'

'I shall let you know.'

'Hmm! And don't try any disappearing tricks yourself, or I'll have a warrant for your arrest before you can get to the nearest bus stop.'

'I bet he does know where she is,' Adderly said, as they went down in the lift.

'Of course he does. Yorkshire, indeed! She's probably within a couple of miles of South Ken station.' Sweet paused. 'The question is, how much of what he's told us is fact and how much fiction?'

'The bit about the drugs ties up with what I learnt after Arne's trial. My bet is that Kapur himself was also involved.'

'Probably.'

'In which event, Kapur had a motive for the murder. It struck me that he was almost too anxious to slide the shit into Francis Arne's lap.'

'I know. We've obviously got to have another go at young Arne.' Sweet grimaced. 'Pity I feel obliged to let Rosa Epton in on the act.'

'You could make some excuse, sir.'

'I could, but I shan't,' Sweet said firmly. In a thoughtful tone he went on, 'If Kapur did murder Philip Arne, why should he have sent his girl-friend round to the flat a few hours later? It was a risky thing to do and there must have been a compelling reason.'

'He wanted to make sure he'd left no clues behind.'

Sweet shook his head. 'Surely he'd have seen to that himself while he was there. Murderers don't usually return to the scene to clear up; or, in this instance, send their girlfriend round. That's the bit I find hardest to accept if he was in fact the murderer. On the other hand, he may well have believed that a murder had taken place and he wanted to make sure that nothing could be found to implicate him in any criminal enterprise.'

'Such as drug-trafficking you mean, sir?'

'Yes.' Sweet paused. 'In fact, most of what he told us may have been true, but it was heavily slanted in his favour.'

'One thing for sure,' Adderly remarked, 'Nadia Beresford, when we do catch up with her, will support him to the hilt. There's nothing we can do to prevent him rehearsing her in what she's going to say.'

'I shall still put the fear of God into her when we do eventually meet.'

Adderly had seldom heard his chief inspector sound so full of grim relish.

CHAPTER 23

Shiv Kapur's telephone rang within a few minutes of the officers' departure.

He walked over to answer it with a set expression.

'It's me, darling. I'm lonely and missing you,' Nadia cooed down the line.

'I particularly told you not to call me,' he replied furiously. 'I said I'd ring you.'

'I know you did, darling, but I really am missing you.'

'Do you realise the police have only just left?' he went on in the same tone of controlled fury. 'If they'd still been here, I daren't think what might have happened.'

'The police? What did they want?'

'They were looking for you. Rosa Epton obviously contacted them immediately. I suspected she would.'

'What did you tell them?' she asked in a small, frightened voice.

'In the first place, I told them that I didn't know where you were. I said you'd gone up to Yorkshire and forgotten to leave a phone number. But I was also forced to tell them that you did go to Philip's flat and how you found him dead. There was no mileage in lying about that any longer. The only course was to come clean and give things as innocent an explanation as I could. I told them I sent you round, as I was worried when Philip didn't answer his phone, and that you were only there a few minutes as a result of what you discovered.'

'I'm scared, Shiv,' she said.

'There's no need to be. Just keep your head and do as I tell you and it'll be all right.'

'When can I see you?'

'You can come back tomorrow morning and I'll have to let Chief Inspector Sweet know.'

'Can't I be with you tonight, darling?' she asked in a pleading tone.

'No. And if you want to go on being my little princess, I don't want you to question what I tell you.'

'I won't. I promise I won't.'

'Good! When you get back I'll tell you exactly what you have to say to the police.'

'They don't think I had anything to do with the murder?' she asked anxiously.

'I hope I've succeeded in sending them off on a fresh scent.'

CHAPTER 24

Francis lay fully dressed on top of his bed, where nowadays he seemed to spend even more of his time than previously. Beside him sat Perry perched like an anxious mother with her sick child. From time to time he put out a hand and gently caressed his friend's brow.

'God, what a mess my life is!' Francis muttered in a tone of deepest gloom.

'It's not that bad. You were acquitted and those two officers are obviously in for it. I know you're upset about your brother's death, but ...'

'You don't know half of it,' Francis broke in abrasively.

'Half of what? I only know what you tell me. Why don't you tell me more? You know you can trust me. I've proved that to you.'

Francis nodded grudgingly. 'I know and I've been pretty bloody to you in return. The truth is,' he went on with a sour little smile, 'I'm not a very nice person to know.'

'I think you are.'

'Which shows you're a nutcase.' This time his tone carried a note of amused tolerance.

Perry smiled happily at the accolade. It was rare, indeed, for Francis to show even that amount of caring.

'Why don't we leave London and go away somewhere together?' he said.

'Where?'

'Anywhere. It doesn't matter. Anywhere you like.'

'And what do we use for money?'

'I've got a bit saved up.'

'It wouldn't be any good.'

'Why not? A fresh ...'

'You don't know what you're saying.' Francis turned his face toward the wall. 'I'm in the muck up to my chin and going away won't help. It'll only make things worse.'

Perry stared at the back of his friend's head with a worried frown.

'In what way are you in the muck, as you put it?'

'In every way. Now stop asking me questions!'

'I wish you'd tell me.'

'Well I won't, so don't hassle me!'

'If you won't talk to me, why not go and get it off your chest to Miss Epton?'

'Are you crazy?'

'You're not worried that ... about your own position ..?'

'What are you trying to say now for heaven's sake?'

Perry took a deep breath. 'I mean, about the police and Philip's murder ... you're not worried they may suspect you?'

'How do I know?'

'But if you didn't ...' The sentence petered out in an anguished silence on Perry's part.

'Didn't what?'

'It doesn't matter.'

'Didn't have anything to do with the murder; that's what you were going to ask, wasn't it?'

'Perhaps.'

Francis turned his head and gave his friend a lopsided grin. 'How does it feel sitting on a bed with a murderer?'

'Don't say things like that. I won't believe you.'

'That's all right then.'

'You were joking, weren't you?'

'Sure, I was joking.'

'After all, you had no motive for murdering your brother,' Perry went on, as if compelled to pick at a sore.

'I'm getting bored with this conversation,' Francis said abruptly. 'Go and make me a coffee.'

131

As Perry moved about the kitchen, his mind alternated between two scenarios. In one, he was proving Francis' innocence to the world. The other saw him faithfully visiting his friend in prison every month for the next decade.

If only Francis would take him more into his confidence ...

Perhaps he, Perry, should go and see Rosa Epton and invoke her help. She had seemed a sympathetic person and would surely give him a hearing. But what exactly did he expect her to do? He even considered the possibility of broaching the formidable father from whom Francis was estranged, but what precisely would he say to him? A sympathetic reception in that quarter seemed as likely as one from a tigress with cubs. On the other hand anything was worth trying for Francis' sake.

He returned to the bedroom with a mug of coffee to find Francis apparently asleep, though he was never too sure when he was genuinely so or when he was feigning.

He put the mug down on the floor beside the bed and retreated. A minute or two later he tiptoed out of the house and made his way to the public call box at the end of the road. Luckily he had earlier made a note of Rosa's number, so he didn't have to try and find it in one of the eviscerated directories.

To his gratification, he was quickly put through to Rosa herself who said that if he could come along immediately, she would be free to see him before she went off to an afternoon court.

'It's very kind of you to say I could come and see you, Miss Epton,' Perry said, as soon as he was seated in her office. 'I thought you were terrific when you defended Francis and he's tremendously grateful to you,' he went on eagerly.

Rosa raised a wry eyebrow. 'I can't quite see him demonstrating tremendous gratitude to anyone,' she remarked.

'He often finds it hard to say what he really feels.'

'I'll take your word for it. Anyway, what brings you to see me?'

Perry's expression clouded over. 'I'm very worried about him. He's definitely got something on his mind, but he refuses to talk. He just lies listlessly on his bed most of the day. Would it be possible for you to speak to him and find out what's troubling him?'

'If he won't talk to you, Perry, I'm sure he won't to me. After all, you're a friend, I'm only his lawyer. And at the moment I'm not even that. My professional responsibility toward him ended with the case, though I'd certainly look after his interests again if he wished.'

'You mean if he was charged with his brother's murder?'

Rosa looked at him sharply. 'I hope there won't be any question of that.'

'So do I.'

'But presumably you had some reason for suggesting that he might be?'

Perry shook his head forlornly. 'I'm sure he never killed Philip, but when I've tried to draw him out and get him to protest his innocence he's evaded the issue, and it made me wonder . . .'

'I see.'

'But the main thing is that he and Philip got on well and he can't have had any motive for murdering him,' he said in a brighter voice.

Rosa recalled the row with his brother to which Francis had referred, though steadfastly refusing to tell her what it was about.

Rows could lead to murder, especially frenzied murders such as this had been.

'I don't think there's anything I can do to help at the moment, Perry,' she said after a thoughtful pause.

He nodded sadly. 'I understand. I'm sorry if I've wasted your time.'

133

'That's the last thing you've done. It's been nice meeting you again and Francis is lucky to have such a staunch friend. I'm afraid he's a very mixed-up young person.'

'Most of us are. Mixed up one way or another, I mean.'

Rosa smiled. 'I'll go along with that view,' she remarked. In a more practical tone she added, 'As a matter of fact, if the police do decide to question him further about his brother's death, the officer in charge has promised to let me know so that I can be present and advise him on his rights.'

'Oh, I am relieved to hear that,' Perry said with obvious delight. 'That really puts my mind at rest.' After a short silence, he added, 'I wonder who did murder Philip? What's your theory, Miss Epton?'

Rosa shook her head and shrugged. Whatever theory she had she was keeping to herself for the time being.

CHAPTER 25

When Rosa returned to her office from court around four-thirty, it was to be told by Stephanie that Detective Chief Inspector Sweet had called, also a Lieutenant Colonel Arne who had left a Worthing number.

'He sounded like a peppery old colonel, too.' Stephanie observed.

Rosa tried to phone Sweet immediately, but he was out and nobody seemed to know when he would be back.

If he was out, at least he couldn't be interrogating Francis, Rosa reflected. Moreover she was sure that if the police did suddenly pick him up for further questioning, Perry would hot-foot it to the nearest telephone before they reached the end of the street.

As for Colonel Arne, she wondered what on earth he had to say to her and it was with mixed feelings that she dutifully dialled his number.

The voice that answered was just as Stephanie had described. Briskly formal and unwelcoming.

'My name's Rosa Epton. I understand you called me earlier this afternoon when I was out.'

'Miss Epton, the solicitor?' he enquired, as though prototypes abounded.

'Yes.'

'I believe you recently defended my son on some charge before the magistrates and got him off?'

'Yes.' Rosa's tone was wary. She had no intention of discussing her client's affairs with any third party, least of all his father.

'I know that doesn't necessarily mean he was innocent, but I should like to thank you.'

'I was glad to be able to help him,' she remarked in a tone that almost matched his for dispassion.

'What I really wanted to say, Miss Epton, is that I'm prepared to help defray the costs of his defence.'

'There aren't any. He was on legal aid.'

'You mean he was defended at the taxpayer's expense?'

'Yes, as are most of the people who appear in criminal courts.'

After a slight pause, Colonel Arne said awkwardly, 'I expect you know we're not on very good terms?'

'So I gathered.'

'But there's no occasion for me to concern you with the background to all that.' So why refer to it at all, Rosa wondered? Colonel Arne went on, 'I suppose you know that my older son has been murdered?'

'Yes, I'd met Philip a few times and was very sorry about his death.'

'My life seems to have fallen apart recently, what with my wife's death and now all this.' His voice trembled momentarily, but he soon had it under control again. 'Detective Chief Inspector Sweet came to see me a little while ago. Do you know him?'

'Yes.'

'Competent officer, is he?'

'I'd say so,' Rosa replied, still puzzled by the twists of their conversation.

'He didn't seem to have any idea who'd done it.'

'I think they're stuck for a motive.'

'I can see that makes their job more difficult. This may sound a rather curious thing to say, Miss Epton, but it's very disturbing to think of one's son's murderer still being at large.'

'I can understand that.'

'Very unsettling, indeed! Particularly as I gather the police rule out a casual intruder and are sure it must have been someone within his circle of acquaintances.'

'I agree it's a disagreeable thought.'

'I certainly find it so.' There was another awkward pause before he went on, 'If I'm starting to talk out of turn, Miss Epton, you must tell me, but I feel I must say what's on my mind.' A further uncomfortable pause followed. 'As far as you're aware, is there any question of Philip's younger brother being suspected?'

'You mean Francis?' Rosa said, momentarily taken aback by the odd piece of circumlocution.

'Yes.'

'The police have certainly questioned him, along with a great number of other people,' she said cautiously. 'But that's all.'

'You don't think they seriously suspect him?'

'I'm afraid I'm not in their confidence.'

'Are you still acting as his solicitor?'

'Yes, you could say that.'

'Good, I'm glad. Whatever I may feel about him, he is my son and I wouldn't want him to face anything as serious as that without professional help.' He was silent for a moment. 'I'm sorry to have taken up your time, Miss Epton. We may not have been a united or a happy family where the boys were concerned, but I'm not a completely heartless person – though you may have been led to believe otherwise. May I ask you to let me know if anything happens to Francis? Incidentally, I'd prefer it if you didn't say anything to him about my call. He wouldn't understand.'

Rosa wasn't too sure that she did herself.

After two further attempts to reach Chief Inspector Sweet on the telephone, each time to be told that he was still out, she decided to go home.

She couldn't think what reason Sweet might have had for calling her other than about Francis, but she trusted him not to go back on his word to let her know if the police wished to question him again. If that had been the purpose of his call, obviously something more important had come up in the meantime.

She left a message for him so that he would at least know she had tried to return his call.

She had just filled her briefcase with papers to study at home when her phone rang.

'It's that funny little chap again,' Stephanie said. 'You know, Perry.'

'Here in the office, you mean?'

'No, on the line. He sounds upset and wants to speak to you, but I told him I wasn't sure if you were still here, so if you'd sooner not ...'

'No, put him through, Stephanie, I'll see what he wants.'

A few seconds later an agitated Perry was on the line.

'It's Perry, Miss Epton. I'm terribly sorry to bother you again, but I'm so worried about Francis. He's disappeared.'

'You'd better explain.'

'Well, when I got back from seeing you this morning, he wasn't in his room. Dave – he's the artist – said Francis had gone out about half an hour after I'd left and he hasn't been seen since.'

'That's hardly evidence of disappearance,' Rosa said robustly.

'He's been gone for over five hours.'

'Most likely he's out on one of his long walks. I'm sure he'll be back later on.'

'But supposing he's not?'

Rosa sighed. 'There'll be time to deal with that situation when it arises.'

'May I phone you in the morning if he's still missing?'

'By all means,' Rosa replied, though wondering what she could be expected to do.

'I'm sorry to be such a nuisance.'

'That's all right. I realise you're worried, but there really is nothing to be done. I'm sure he's all right. After all, I'd have been told if the police had taken him in.'

'It's been a real comfort talking to you, Miss Epton,' Perry said gratefully.

'I'm glad I've managed to allay your fears.'

'I'll call you in the morning.'

'Only if he's still missing.'

'Won't you want to know if he's back?'

'I'll assume it,' she said firmly.

As she picked up her briefcase and made for the door, she reflected on the Perrys of this life, who went on displaying loyal friendship in the face of discouragement and rebuffs. It was a quality of doglike devotion she found touching and which accounted for her willingness to give him more of her unpaid time than could ever be justified by any computerised cost-effectiveness.

CHAPTER 26

Detective Chief Inspector Sweet's protracted absence from his station had been occasioned by a phone call from Detective Inspector Parrish, as a result of which the two men met on the neutral ground of Scotland Yard. Or to be more precise in the office of Detective Inspector Newman of C.13, a branch of the C.I.D. that interested itself in a mixed bag known as Special Crimes.

'We originally got our tip-off from C.11,' Newman said, referring to the department's central intelligence branch, and looking from one to the other of his two visitors with the faintly worried air of someone not too sure of his popularity. 'For obvious reasons, we've had to work very much under cover or we shouldn't have got anywhere. As it is, our enquiry still has some way to go before we'll be ready to confront Kapur with what we've found out. We obviously don't want him to get wind of anything and take fright.'

'Another bloody case of the right hand not knowing what the left is up to,' Parrish said vigorously.

Inspector Newman gave him a pained look. 'I can't see that it can be otherwise at times,' he remarked. 'The need to know is always the soundest principle to work on in our sort of operations.'

Parrish let out a scornful grunt. 'I'd have thought Chief Inspector Sweet and myself would have been let in on the secret, seeing that Kapur works from an office on my manor and is a suspect in Mr Sweet's murder enquiry.'

Inspector Newman nodded owlishly.

'With hindsight, it is perhaps unfortunate that you weren't, but I assure you that our enquiry was never likely to queer your pitch.'

'I don't know how you can say that!' Sweet observed. 'And anyway, ours might have queered yours.'

'On the contrary, your murder enquiry was seen as a useful lightning conductor so far as we were concerned. It diverted Kapur's attention. Obviously we shouldn't try and prevent you arresting him for murder once you have a case, though our own investigation will have to continue in view of its ramifications. All I would ask is that you have a word with me before moving against him.'

'I propose to interview him again very shortly,' Sweet said. 'Even if I don't yet have enough to charge him, he's still very much in the frame as a suspect. And there's his girl-friend, too.'

'Ah yes, Miss Beresford,' Newman remarked with a thoughtful nod.

'Is she involved with your enquiry?'

'We're not yet sure how much, if anything, she knew of what was going on.'

'Well, she certainly knows something about Philip Arne's murder and I intend to find out what,' Sweet added with grim determination.

'Wonderful, isn't it!' Parrish observed later in a soothing tone when he and Sweet were ensconced in a nearby pub. 'It was pure chance I caught word about C.13's enquiry, other-wise we'd still have been in pig ignorance.'

'They clearly don't consider it touches on Arne's murder.'

'They mayn't, but are you so sure, Tom?'

'No, I'm not.'

'There you are then! If Arne and Kapur were such bosom friends and also worked under the same shady umbrella, it's more than likely that Arne was involved in the racket.'

Sweet nodded solemnly. The news that Shiv Kapur was under investigation for selling false passports, complete with entry stamps, to illegal immigrants had come as a complete surprise to him. It more than accounted for Kapur's affluence, for, from what Inspector Newman had said, it was a racket involving tens of thousands of pounds a year, as well as a national network in those parts of the country where Asian immigrants tended to congregate.

It was, indeed, difficult to believe that Philip Arne had not played a part. And if he had, it followed that a motive for his murder could lie buried somewhere in those murky dealings.

As he drove back to his station, Tom Sweet tried to decide which line of enquiry should now receive priority.

At his recent interview with the police, Kapur had subtly insinuated that Francis Arne had murdered his brother following a quarrel over the drugs deal that had gone seriously wrong. Though Kapur certainly had every reason to try and divert attention away from himself, there was, nevertheless, independent confirmation of the drugs story.

So perhaps Francis Arne had better remain at the head of his list. He had tried to call Rosa Epton before being summoned to the Yard. By now she would have left her office. He would call her at home and, if she wasn't there, well it might be necessary to pick Arne up anyway and bring him along to the station. The only thing was that he'd be unlikely to say anything unless she were present.

Sweet sighed. It was at moments like these that early retirement seemed such an attractive prospect.

CHAPTER 27

When Francis heard Perry leave the flat, he realised it was his opportunity to slip out himself without being questioned, or, worse still, followed.

His one idea was to walk. It mattered not where, but just walk. It would help to clear his head which, at this moment, seethed with a miasma of frightening thoughts. He was gripped by a fear, made worse by the fact he had nobody to talk to. Perry longed to be his confidant, but what could Perry do to help? His sympathetic noises would merely be an irritant and cause him, Francis, to say hurtful things. And he could hardly go and lay all his fears and anxieties on Rosa Epton's desk. After all, she could only offer him lawyer's advice which was probably the last thing he wanted to hear.

And yet the urge to talk to somebody had suddenly become overwhelming. Ever since his arrest in Kenpark Square he had been bottling up his worries and now carried within him an explosive mixture of dark emotions.

It crossed his mind how cleansing it would be to lie on a couch in a psychiatrist's shaded consulting room and pour out his troubles to a detached, professional listener who would know exactly how to respond. It was a picture that came to him like a mirage of cool water to a desert traveller mad with thirst.

He gave a derisive grunt as he summarily dismissed it from his mind and quickened his pace with a spurious air of purposefulness.

Turning into Kensington Gardens, he went and sat under a tree for a few minutes. Then, restless, he got up and moved on again. The prospect of having to return to the flat in

Hammersmith filled him with dread. But where else could he go? If only Philip were still alive!

He supposed later it must have been his subconscious that guided him there, but he became aware that he was not far from where Shiv Kapur lived. He had been there only once before, to a party with Philip, though he had met Kapur several times at Philip's flat in Clapham.

He recalled how Kapur had turned up at court and spoken to him sympathetically afterwards, how he had been a close friend of Philip's, and how, only the other day, he had extended what he called a hand of brotherly love which waited to be grasped whenever he, Francis, felt the need. That particularly flowery invitation had followed their meeting in court.

He arrived at the block of flats and pushed the bell, without really expecting a reply. A few seconds later, however, the Indian's disembodied voice crackled through the answer-phone.

'It's Francis, Shiv. I'd like to see you.'

'Francis ... Francis ... Yes, of course, please come up. I'm on the sixth floor. I'll buzz the door so that you can get in.'

When Francis stepped out of the lift, Shiv Kapur was standing at his open front door with a welcoming smile on his face.

'I'm sorry if I sounded surprised. As a matter of fact, I was expecting somebody else.'

'Would you like me to leave then?'

Kapur raised his hands in a deprecatory gesture. 'Leave? The brother of my dearest friend! That I could be thought so inhospitable!'

'I just have to talk to somebody.'

'I'm honoured that I should be the recipient of your confidence.'

'I'm so worried; I don't really know where to begin.' He paused and bit his lip hard. 'I believe you know that Philip dabbled a bit with drugs?'

Kapur nodded gravely. 'Yes. It was naughty of him and naughtier still to involve you.'

'You knew that?'

'Yes, but it is a secret I shall share with no one.'

'Then I suppose you know why I was in Kenpark Square that evening?'

'Philip told me. He was very upset at what happened.'

'He was absolutely livid. He said I'd bungled a deal it had taken him weeks to set up. We lost everything. Sombody obviously tipped off the police.'

'It was a most unhappy episode for you,' Kapur said in a sorrowful tone. 'And that it should have happened the night before poor Philip's death! That you should have been left with such a tragic memory!'

'You don't think that I murdered Philip, do you?' Francis said sharply.

Kapur held up a placatory hand. 'I know you could not have. The brotherly bonds that held you together would not have permitted such a dastardly deed.'

'Who do you think did kill him?'

'It couldn't have been anyone who loved him as we did.'

'But the police are sure it wasn't a casual intruder.' Francis looked up and met Kapur's steady gaze. 'I suppose they've questioned you?'

'I have given them every assistance I can.' He paused and laid a hand delicately on Francis' forearm. 'It is providence that has brought you here today, I think.'

'What do you mean?'

'The police were here last night and asked many questions about you.' Observing Francis' alarmed expression, he went on in a reassuring voice, 'I told them nothing, of course, save that it was unthinkable you had anything to do with Philip's death.'

'What sort of questions did they ask?'

145

'How you and Philip got on? Might you have had a motive for murdering him? It was questions, questions, all about you and Philip ... But I told them what a lovely relationship you enjoyed ... Nevertheless ...' Kapur paused and stared thoughtfully at his guest for several seconds. 'Nevertheless, it might be better if you went away for a short while. You have been through an ordeal and would benefit from a rest. You need to get away and forget. Otherwise I fear very much that the police may start harassing you again over Philip's death ... wearing you down with their questions.'

'That's all very fine, Shiv, but where the hell can I go?' His tone was bitter.

Kapur gave him an indulgent smile. 'What is a friend for, but to help at a time of need. I would be happy to arrange a little holiday for you.'

'Where?' Francis said suspiciously.

'I have some dear friends who would look after you for a while and protect you against harassment.'

'Where do they live?'

'On a farm in Warwickshire. It is very lovely there and you would find it most restful after all you've been through.' He glanced at his watch. 'It wouldn't take me long to make the arrangements and you could go immediately. It would be the best thing for you. To get right away.'

Francis looked doubtful. 'Suppose the police start looking for me. They'll think I've run away because I'm guilty.'

'How could they think such nonsense! If they want to talk to you, they will wait till you come back to London. You're not disappearing or going missing; you're just taking a break from all the pressures that have built up. I'd worry for your health if you didn't go away.' He leaned forward and said earnestly, 'Now, let me fetch you a drink and while you are relaxing, I will go and make arrangements. Since it is all decided, the sooner you go the better. And perhaps while you're resting, the case will be solved.' He reached for a slim black leather wallet which lay on the low table in front of him and pulled out five £20 notes. 'Here, take this!'

Francis accepted the money and watched Kapur get up and walk toward the door. His expression gave as little away as the Indian's.

CHAPTER 28

'I wish I had broken the little shit's arm. And his flaming neck!' P.C. Paynter remarked viciously as he and Hexham sat, off duty, in a corner of a pub outside their station area.

'We don't even know if he's made a complaint,' Hexham said.

'He'll jump on the bandwagon quick enough, aided and abetted by that female solicitor of his.'

'What do you think's going to happen, Terry?' Hexham asked in a worried tone.

'Somehow or other our people have got wind of that drugs deal, which means we're in the muck for not having reported it.' Hexham noted the "we" with some bitterness, but refrained from comment. 'If everything had gone according to plan, we'd have been receiving commendations, instead of facing suspension.'

'I suppose we're bound to be suspended while they investigate,' Hexham said in an utterly dispirited voice.

'Once they've latched onto the drugs deal, they'll go and see Arne, who'll shoot his mouth at our expense. That means a full scale investigation of what happened that evening and the odds are we'll be suspended from duty pending its outcome.'

Hexham shook his head forlornly. He had never had the stomach for a fight and was in no mood to reproach his companion for having landed him in this frightening mess.

'If only you hadn't let the other chap get away,' Paynter added rancorously.

Hexham let out a weary sigh, but still said nothing. He wished he could quietly resign instead of facing the humiliation of being asked to leave the force, *or*. And that was likely to be the best which could happen. He shrank from contemplating the worst.

As if reading his thoughts, Paynter went on remorselessly, 'Of course, we could be done for perjury and attempting to pervert the course of justice. It's as well to know that.' He paused and stared grimly into his empty glass. 'Trouble is we're expected to fight crime with one arm tied behind our backs. As long as you get results, nobody asks too many questions, but come unstuck and they're ready to tear you apart, tell you you've been a naughty boy and all that crap. Arne was bloody lucky to get away with a sus charge when we all know he should have been on a much more serious one.'

'He'd still have fought it all the way.'

'Because he's a vicious little brat,' Paynter said, while Hexham tried to follow the logic of his companion's comment. 'And anyway,' he added belligerently, 'he wasn't framed. He did touch the door of the Rolls.'

'He never went near the Mercedes.'

'Bugger the Mercedes! That's what I'm saying; succeed and nobody asks any questions; fail and out come the scalpels. The Mercedes bit was a necessary gilding of the lily. So what! Does the public want protection from its criminals or not? What we did goes on all the time, so don't get all uptight with me, Peter Hexham.'

'I wasn't.'

'You'd better not. We're in this together and that means a fight. I'll fight any allegations Arne makes to the bitter end and you're going to fight alongside me. All we've got to do is deny that anything improper took place. And go on denying. They can't have any proof.'

'Arne. He's the proof.'

'Who's going to accept his word?' Paynter said explosively.

'The magistrate did.'

'Balls! He merely found that the prosecution hadn't proved its case beyond reasonable doubt, which isn't the same thing at all. And whose fault was that? If we'd had a decent prosecuting solicitor instead of that wet they sent along, it could have been a very different story. That bloke should never have been let loose in a court.' Paynter fixed his colleague with a long, hard gaze. 'Of course, the best thing that could happen to us would be for Arne to be charged with his brother's murder.' After a thoughtful pause, he added, 'Pity we've no way of fixing that.' Observing Hexham's look of horror, he went on, 'No need to break out in a sweat! I was only thinking out aloud. All I know is that if I was the officer in charge and was sure he'd done it, I'd set about giving the evidence a bit of a nudge in the right direction. That's where you and I are different, Pete, I go out and attack while you sit back and wait.'

Peter Hexham could think of other differences, but was too far sunk in despair to enter into an argument. That was the trouble with the likes of Terry Paynter, you either went along unquestioningly with everything he said and suggested, or you became locked in controversy, from which he was determined to emerge the victor.

All right, maybe you did need a touch of ruthlessness to succeed as a police officer, but being unscrupulous was something different.

'A penny for your thoughts,' Paynter remarked suddenly.

Hexham started guiltily. 'They're not worth that,' he said with a weak smile.

'Then pay attention to me while I tell you what we've got to say when we're questioned. It's important to get it right, as they'll almost certainly tackle you before me. It's natural to probe the weakest spot first . . .'

CHAPTER 29

'I'm calling from the railway station,' Shiv Kapur said. 'He's on the train, so make sure you meet him.'

'Is this a good idea?' his brother, Prasad, asked doubtfully.

'It's important to have him away from London and out of reach of the police for a time,' Kapur said emphatically. 'I explained that when I phoned from the flat.'

'I know you explained, but is it a good idea sending him here?'

'Providing you keep a close eye on him, brother, and don't give him the run of the place, no harm can befall us.'

'Supposing he starts poking his nose where he shouldn't?'

'You must see that he doesn't. I think he will be in the mood to do anything you tell him.'

'I'm still not happy that he's coming.'

Shiv Kapur sighed. 'I couldn't think of anywhere else in the time available.'

'It's a pity he's coming.'

'So you've made clear, but you have to back me up. Incidentally, I don't want you to call me at the flat. The police may be tapping my line.'

'Now you tell me that! Next you will say they are on the train with him.'

'Calm yourself, brother! You're safe and sound up on the farm. It's I at the pointed end of our affairs. Anyway, I'm not saying the line is tapped, though I think it may be soon. They're trying to trace Nadia. It's one of the reasons I'm phoning from Euston Station.'

'Nadia!' Prasad said in a tone of angry scorn.

'I know you don't like her, but she does have her uses.'

'In your bed, I suppose.'

Kapur giggled. 'Out of it as well.'

'She could become a danger, if she hasn't already.'

'You can rely on me, brother, to make sure she doesn't.'

'I have to. Meanwhile, I had better make sure there is nothing here to arouse the suspicions of the visitor you're sending me.'

'Providing you don't give him keys to any locked doors, everything will be all right. It is I in London, caught up in this damnable murder investigation that am facing problems.'

'But now you wish to involve me in your London problems. I had nothing to do with Philip's death, but you are sending his brother here to keep him away from the police. Soon my problems will be as great as yours.'

Kapur sighed heavily. His brother, who was eight years older than himself, had always been a confirmed pessimist. He was grave and suspicious where Shiv was mercurial and ever adjusting to each situation as it arose. But Prasad was also an unbreakable rock and together they made a formidable partnership. He, Shiv, had the entrepreneurial skills and Prasad was the perfect works manager, being infinitely careful and discreet over every detail.

For it was in the basement of the the lonely Warwickshire farmhouse that the home-made presses turned out forged passports and other documents that were such a profitable line of business.

'Your problems will never be as great as mine, brother,' Shiv now said in a consoling voice. 'You are too wise.'

'Not so wise that I don't have a brother like you. Anyway, who did murder Philip? Is it not time the police arrested the culprit?'

'Yes, indeed, brother, let us hope sincerely that they soon will make an arrest,' Shiv Kapur said in a tone that did honour to the Delphic oracle.

The telephone indicated its impatient need of further

coins and Shiv rang off after a final exhortation to his brother to be sure to be at the station in good time.

Two and a half hours later, however, despite his brother's fear of the possibility of his line being tapped, a dour and uneasy Prasad felt compelled to call Shiv and tell him that Francis had never arrived.

CHAPTER 30

Rosa had barely arrived in her office the next morning when she received two telephone calls in quick succession.

The first came from a pathetically worried Perry who told her that he had lain awake all night listening in vain for his friend's return. He reminded her that Francis had now been missing for nearly twenty-four hours and asked her what they should do.

'There's nothing we can do, Perry,' she replied kindly, but also firmly.

'But surely there must be something, Miss Epton,' he pleaded.

'What do you suggest?' she asked with a touch of asperity. 'It's hardly a case for rushing to the police.'

'That's the last thing . . .'

'So all we can do is sit tight and wait for news of him. Twenty-four hours isn't very long for a loner like him to disappear. If any harm had befallen him, we'd know.'

'Do you really believe that?' Perry asked, grasping at this tiny straw of comfort.

The trouble was that Rosa didn't necessarily believe it. She didn't quite know what to believe, except that something told her his disappearance wasn't the motiveless act of a wayward young man as she had suggested.

After a few further calming words to Perry, she brought to a conclusion a conversation that, if left to him, would be unlikely, she felt, to reach an end. He promised to let her know as soon as he had any news of Francis.

'And you'll let me know, too, won't you, Miss Epton, if you hear anything first?'

'I have no way of getting in touch with you on the

phone, Perry, so why don't you call me at the end of the afternoon to see if I've heard anything.' Anticipating a suggestion that he should call her every hour through the day, she added firmly, 'I'll be out of the office till then.'

She had hardly replaced the receiver when Stephanie announced that Detective Chief Inspector Sweet was on the line.

'Is that you, Miss Epton?' he asked in a gritty tone. 'I was proposing to have a further interview with your client this morning, but I've just heard that he's gone missing. Where can I find him?'

'I'm afraid I can't tell you; I don't know where he is. I've only heard the news of his disappearance myself within the past five minutes.'

'Oh! and who told you?'

Rosa felt like telling him to mind his own business, but decided it was not the moment to pick a quarrel with the investigating officer of Philip Arne's murder.

'Someone with whom Arne shares a flat,' she said. 'And you, how did you find out?' As Perry had made no mention of the police going to the house, she was curious as to the source of Sweet's knowledge.

'I sent a car to fetch him to the station,' Sweet said, adding quickly, 'and was going to call you as soon as I had him here. One of his flat mates condescended to break off from painting a picture to inform my officer that Arne had gone out yesterday morning and had not been seen since.'

From this Rosa was left to conjecture that Sweet's emissaries had arrived while Perry was out phoning her. That meant he would be back on the line any moment now to tell her what she already knew.

'Was it something particular you wanted to see him about?' she enquired in an innocent tone.

'It was, indeed, Miss Epton. I've recently received further information which throws fresh light on Philip Arne's murder and I have reason to believe that your client can assist me.'

Despite the grimness of its message, the well worn cliché brought a small smile to Rosa's lips. It was clear, however, that Sweet now strongly suspected Francis of killing his brother and was intent on a tough interrogation, at the end of which he would hope to be able to prefer a charge.

'What is the further information you're referring to, Mr Sweet?' she enquired, as though it were the most natural question in the world to ask.

'I'm afraid I'm not prepared to discuss that, Miss Epton,' he replied, as she had expected he would. 'Suffice it to say I want to see Arne urgently and am proposing to put out a general alert for him. Meanwhile, should he suddenly turn up in your office, I rely on you to advise him where his best interests lie and to let me know immediately.'

Rosa reflected wryly how often the police were given to identifying the interests of those they were keen to question with their own, when, in fact, the former might be better advised to hot-foot it to John O'Groats.

After Sweet had rung off, she sat sunk in thought for several minutes, reviewing the situation that had arisen. It was never good for a lawyer to become emotionally involved with clients and nobody was better aware of this than she, it being a precept she had not always found it easy to follow. Moreover, she wasn't emotionally involved so far as Francis was concerned. The fact remained, however, that she had liked his brother more than she cared to admit and had been deeply shaken by his brutal murder, with the result that she now felt herself pulled in various directions. She had gone further than strict duty required by continuing to act for Francis after his case was concluded, even though there was still the question of an unofficial complaint about the conduct of the two P.C.s to be decided. But her brief certainly did not extend to protecting Francis' interests *vis-a-vis* the murder enquiry. Nevertheless, it was what she was doing, not for his sake, so much as out of affection for Philip's memory.

And here she was starkly faced with the prospect of Francis being charged with his brother's murder. The irony of the situation was not lost on her. Having taken Francis under her wing at Philip's request, she could scarcely abandon him if he turned out to be his brother's killer. Professional duty was professional duty, however distasteful it might become.

It was while she was pursuing her somewhat sombre thoughts that her phone buzzed.

'I've got your young man on the line,' Stephanie said. 'He's in a public call box.'

'Perry, do you mean?'

'No, the other one, Francis.'

'Then put him through,' Rosa said, trying to sound calmer that she felt.

'It's me,' Francis said a moment later in his flat monotone.

'Where are you?'

'I want to talk to you, but I can't come to your office. The police might pick me up.'

'Where are you speaking from?'

'A call box on the North Circular. Can I meet you somewhere this evening after dark?'

'Will you come to my flat?'

'Provided it's safe.'

'Of course it is.'

'O.K., I trust you,' he said in a voice in which defiance and desperation were mixed.

'Call me before you arrive and I'll tell you whether the coast is clear. Not that I have the slightest reason to think it won't be. Incidentally, the police are looking for you. Chief Inspector Sweet wants to interview you urgently about your brother's death.'

157

'I can guess why,' he said grimly, and rang off.

Once more Rosa found herself plunged into thought. It was now apparent that Francis had not just been wandering aimlessly for the past twenty-four hours and that something had happened. Something sufficiently dramatic to shake him out of his state of sullen apathy.

Rosa had a day's work ahead of her before she would find out, but she felt that the ice had at last begun to crack and that answers would be forthcoming to a number of inexorable questions.

CHAPTER 31

Somebody who felt even more strongly, and certainly more anxiously, that the climax was approaching was Shiv Kapur. When his brother phoned him to say that Francis had not been on the train, he had received the news with relative equanimity, assuming that he had most probably fallen asleep and been unaware of passing his destination.

Indeed, when Prasad had said, 'He wasn't on the train,' he replied, 'You mean, he didn't get off the train.'

Subsequently, however, he became less easy and by the time he went to bed was distinctly troubled. As he sat brooding on Francis' disappearance, he remembered the strange look he had noticed on his face as he drove him to Euston. It was a look that had incorporated a quota of craftiness. But he had been so certain of Francis' eagerness to be helped that he had ignored what he now saw to be hints of deviousness. Being naturally devious himself, his failure to recognise the signs in Francis vexed him the more.

Early next morning he went out to a nearby call box to phone his brother. He was not expecting reassuring news, nor did he receive any. Prasad was plainly worried and in a mood to nag, so that Shiv Kapur was relieved when they were cut off through his failure to insert more money.

He returned grimly thoughtful to his flat and to his other problem, namely Nadia who had returned in the middle of the night and threatened to make a scene if he didn't let her in.

She was still asleep when he got back and he gazed down at her recumbent form with a mixture of indecision and irritation.

'Wake up,' he said, giving her shoulder a nudge with his naked foot.

She turned drowsily and gave the foot a soft kiss. When she began to kiss each of his toes, he quickly removed his foot from the edge of the bed.

'You must get up.'

'Why? Why don't you come back to bed, darling?'

'Because I'm about to call the police and tell them you're here.'

'The police!' She was bolt upright in a moment.

'I promised to let them know as soon as you returned from your supposed visit to Yorkshire. We've been through all this, so don't be difficult.'

'You don't have to call them yet.'

'Yes, now. I've got to keep in their good books and make them believe I'm co-operating. You know what you have to say, so there's nothing to worry about.' He paused and gave her a faintly malicious smile. 'Anyway, it's your fault for coming back before I told you.'

'They'll accuse me of murdering Philip,' she said in an agitated voice.

'No they won't. They haven't any evidence. They'll be angry with you for not reporting the murder, but that's all. Anyway, I shall be beside you. I'm going to tell them you're unwell and they must come here if they wish to see you.' He turned to go and telephone.

'Kiss me,' she said, holding out her arms.

With a small complacent smile, he knelt beside the bed and put his lips to hers. With an anguished cry, she flung her arms around his neck and clung to him.

It was five minutes before he extracted himself from her embrace and a further half hour before Detective Chief Inspector Sweet and Detective Sergeant Adderly arrived on the doorstep. By this time Nadia was dressed in a cream blouse and black skirt and was looking pale and demure.

'As I explained on the telephone, detective inspector,' Kapur said with a disarming smile, 'if Miss Beresford had not been feeling unwell, I'd have brought her to the station.'

'She may still end up there,' Sweet replied, in no mood to be disarmed. He turned to the girl. 'When did you get back?'

'Three o'clock this morning.'

'That's a funny time to return from visiting friends in Yorkshire.'

'I was given a lift and the car broke down,' she said in a voice designed to turn away anger.

'You've been very elusive, haven't you?' She shook her head as though bewildered by the accusation. 'Yes, you have. You've been deliberately avoiding the police.'

'No, I promise you I haven't.'

'You realise you could end up in the dock facing a serious charge?'

She shook her head again like a bewildered child. 'I haven't done anything wrong.'

'You concealed a murder.'

'Is failure to report a crime actually an offence?' Kapur broke in with a tiny gesture of self-deprecation.

'If you don't keep quiet, I'll take you both down to the station,' Sweet said with surprising viciousness.

'I'm sorry, I was only . . .'

'Well don't!'

Trust a bloody Indian to know the law, Sweet thought savagely, his own researches having persuaded him that unless he could prove she had reasonable belief as to who had committed the murder, her failure to report it did not, indeed, constitute an offence.

'You knew Arne was dead when you went to his flat, didn't you?'

'No. I'd never have gone if I'd suspected it.'

'Didn't you go in order to remove any clues the murderer might have left behind?'

'No ... no. It was a terrible shock finding him like that. I was paralysed by fear. My only thought was to flee.'

'So why did you go?'

'Shiv was worried because he couldn't contact Philip on the phone, so he asked me to go round to his flat. You see, he'd talked to Philip on the previous evening and Philip had told him he was about to have a showdown with his brother about something that had happened. He was waiting for his brother to arrive when Shiv spoke to him, but later Shiv couldn't get any answer. Nor when he tried to call him next morning.'

'I think you went back to the flat to remove any clues Shiv left behind when he murdered him the previous evening.'

Kapur frowned. 'Excuse me, chief inspector, but that doesn't make sense. If I'd killed Philip, why would I wait till the next morning – indeed, until there was actual daylight – before sending Miss Beresford there to do what you suggest?'

The logic of this did nothing to improve Sweet's mood. There had been times recently when he felt he was near to the truth, and others, as now, when he seemed as far away as ever.

If, as he now suspected, Philip Arne had been involved in the forged passport racket with Kapur, it opened up a whole vista of unexplored motives. But, to his frustration, this was something he was forbidden to broach for the time being.

Fixing Kapur with a baleful stare, he said suddenly, 'When did you last see Francis Arne?'

'Not since his trial. He's all right, I hope?' he asked in a suddenly anxious tone.

'I never said he wasn't.'

'I was thinking only last night that I ought to get in touch with him. I feel it my duty to keep my eye on him now that

Philip is dead.'

Hypocritical creep, Sweet reflected.

Half an hour later, he and Adderly were on their way back to the station. It seemed to Adderly that his boss had made a right cock-up of the interview and had completely failed to put Nadia through the mill. But then Sergeant Adderly had not been made privy to the wider issues that Sweet was finding so inhibiting.

'Perhaps there'll be news of Arne when we get back,' he said, breaking the dour silence that had descended. 'We've certainly got a lot more now to throw at him.'

But Sweet merely shrugged. In his present mood, all news seemed to be bad news.

CHAPTER 32

It had been dark for over an hour and Francis had still not called her. Despite trying to persuade herself that it would be a relief if he didn't turn up, Rosa was still worried.

His telephone call that morning had unsettled her, being so completely out of character with the Francis she knew. That he wanted to talk to her – indeed, *must* was the word he had used – was evidence of a significant change of attitude. She wondered whether he had undergone some Pauline conversion and was set to treat her to a full confession of his brother's murder. If that was his intention, she could hardly head it off. Like so many situations with which she was confronted both in and out of court, it would be a question of playing it by ear. That was something to which she was well used.

It was while her thoughts were still travelling on these lines that her telephone rang. As soon as she lifted the receiver, she realised that it was somebody in a call box.

After the usual delay while the pips squawked urgently like hungry fledglings and coins were inserted to make a sound like a metallic tummy rumble, his voice came through.

'It's me. O.K. to come along?'

'Yes, I've been expecting you for some time. Where are you?'

'At the end of the road. I'll come now.'

A few minutes later she released the street door to let him in and listened to his footsteps as he climbed the three flights of stairs.

She was waiting at her open front-door when he reached the landing. He walked straight past her and into the flat.

'No problems with the police?' he asked as she closed the door behind him.

'No, they haven't been in touch with me all day.'

A fact for which she had been considerably grateful, seeing the embarrassment a call from Sweet might have caused her. She gave him a quick glance. 'Have you had any-thing to eat?'

He nodded. 'I'm O.K.'

She had, in fact, noticed that he bore less resemblance than usual to a fugitive from justice. 'A tea or coffee, then?'

'I wouldn't mind a coffee.' He stood in the kitchen door and watched her prepare it. 'The real thing, eh?' he remarked in a faintly mocking tone. 'I didn't know anyone drank real coffee any more.'

'I happen to have some left over from last night when a friend came round,' she said, and promptly felt annoyed with herself for feeling obliged to provide an explanation.

He watched her put everything on a tray, but made no offer to carry it.

When they reached the living-room he glanced around and said, 'Where do you want me to sit?'

'Anywhere you like. Face the light, back to the light, take your choice.'

He selected an upright chair near the table on which he put the cup of coffee she handed him.

'Shall I begin?'

'When you're ready.'

'I went to see Shiv Kapur yesterday morning,' he said, grimacing with distaste. 'Don't ask me why! I just wanted to talk to somebody and he and Philip were close friends. Also he'd said he was available should I ever need any help.' He paused and frowned into his cup. 'For a while, I was fooled by that soft talk of his, but then it suddenly dawned on me, he was trying to set me up. He was proposing to frame me, if he could, for Philip's murder. And the answer was, he could. He obviously wanted to deflect police attention away from himself.' He paused again. 'But before I go into all that, I think I'd better come clean about the charge you defended me on. It was a frame-up all right, though I was probably lucky to get away altogether.'

Rosa listened without a flicker of emotion as he described the drugs deal in which he had played a part and which had gone so drastically wrong.

'I'm both surprised and sorry to hear that Philip was mixed up in that sort of thing,' she said, when he had finished.

'But neither surprised nor sorry that I was?' he enquired in a voice that again mocked her.

'You were a good deal luckier than you deserved to be. Not that I have any sympathy with the police for trying to frame you.'

'I should hope not. It was real villainy on their part. They committed downright perjury.'

'The less you say about perjury, the better,' Rosa remarked.

He gave her a quick, lop-sided grin. 'Are you angry with me for telling you the truth?'

She decided that this was not a question she wished to answer at that moment, particularly as she had yet to learn the real purpose of his visit. This came almost with his next breath.

'While I was at Shiv's flat, I had a bit of a look around. He was telephoning in another room, so I knew I wouldn't be disturbed. I happened to open a drawer and . . . well, I now know who murdered Philip and why.'

CHAPTER 33

Beneath his normal passive exterior lurked an extremely worried Shiv Kapur.

It was not long after Sweet and Adderly had departed that Prasad phoned to say he had just learnt from one of their contacts in Wolverhampton that the police had been making enquiries into the sale of forged documents to illegal immigrants. The contact had indicated that the enquiry was no mere local affair, but part of a major investigation.

Shiv had railed at his brother for telephoning him at the flat after being explicitly warned of the danger of so doing, but Prasad had been unrepentant and declared it was a risk he had to take. It had been an urgent necessity to get in touch, so how else?

Shiv was still brooding on the import of this news when Nadia came into the room and flung her arms round his neck from behind. He shook her off roughly.

'I've no time for that now,' he said.

'But, darling, I want to help you. I can tell you're worried so let your little princess smooth away your cares.' She began to nuzzle the back of his neck.

'Go away!' he hissed furiously. 'Go away before I strike you.'

For a moment she stared at him aghast. He had never before spoken to her in that tone nor threatened her with violence and her response was to burst into tears.

He stared at her with hatred. 'Can't you see I'm all on edge?' he said through clenched teeth.

'I've always done everything you ever asked me,' she gasped between sobs. 'I've even risked going to prison for you and now you hate me. Well, there are limits to my loyalty as you'll find out. I'll go to the police and tell them the truth.'

'And what is the truth you will tell them?' he asked in a dangerously quiet tone.

'That you sent me to Philip's flat to remove forged passports.'

'It would be an extremely foolish thing to say and would bring you as much trouble as me.'

'Not the way I'd tell it, it wouldn't,' she replied, tearfully defiant.

'And how *would* you tell it?'

She gave a small shrug. 'After all, how do I know you didn't murder Philip?'

He stared at her with a puzzled expression. 'But we were together that evening.'

'You went out for about half an hour just before nine o'clock, remember. How do I know you didn't drive to Clapham, murder Philip and come back here? You could have done that.'

'But you know where I went. I told you. I had to meet somebody and hand over two passports.'

'That's what you told me, but how do I know it's the truth?'

He remained thoughtfully silent for a while. Then he smiled.

'Why are we quarrelling like this? You know how much I love you.'

Her expression melted. 'How much?' she asked in an eager whisper.

'Come into the bedroom and I'll show you and you can smooth away my cares.'

After they had made love, passionate on her part, less spontaneous on his, he lay gazing up at the silver moon and stars that decorated the midnight blue ceiling.

At least he had won her back for the time being. Her threat to denounce him had, however, been a chilling reminder of the extent to which she could hurt him. Moreover, being such a volatile person, she would be capable of saying the dangerous things she had threatened to tell the police.

'What are you thinking, darling?' she asked, breaking in on his sombre thoughts.

'How much I love you,' he replied, running a finger gently round her navel.

In fact his mind was on more practical matters such as whether or not he would have to kill her. It depended on whether he could do it without falling under suspicion.

And if only he knew what had happened to Francis . . .

CHAPTER 34

Still on that same day that had seen Chief Inspector Sweet outpointed in his frustrated interview with Nadia Beresford and Francis make his way to Rosa's flat under cover of darkness, Sweet received a phone call from Detective Inspector Newman of C.13 at Scotland Yard. It came around half past six in the evening.

'Detective Chief Inspector Sweet?' Newman said in his clinical voice. 'I thought I'd let you know we've decided to have Kapur in for questioning. I don't know whether you'd care to be present?'

'When?'

'Tomorrow. Our hand's been rather forced. There's been a leak and if we don't move straightaway, we'll risk losing vital evidence. At the same time we're proposing to obtain search warrants under the Forgery Act in respect of his Kensington flat, the Reynolds-Bailey Trust premises and a farm up in Warwickshire where Kapur's brother lives and where, we believe, a lot of the forged stuff is manufactured.'

'I'd better warn you that Kapur knows his legal rights,' Sweet said with a touch of malice.

'It'll take more than that to deter me,' Newman said confidently. 'We have more on him than you do, even if we are being obliged to jump the gun. Anyway, as it's possible he may say something pertinent to your enquiry, I thought I'd give you the opportunity of attending if you wished.'

'Yes, I'll be there.'

'You'll understand, of course, that it is *our* interview.'

'You've made that clear,' Sweet remarked drily.

'Good. Incidentally, is he more or less of a suspect in your case than he was when we talked a couple of days ago?'

170

'I'm missing only one tiny bit of evidence against him.'

'What's that?'

'I wish I knew.'

Newman let out a small, mirthless laugh.

'If you're as close as that, you're bound to nail him sooner or later.'

'The trouble is that Kapur and young Arne are involved in a photo-finish as far as I'm concerned. Each could have done it and yet ...'

And yet he wasn't satisfied is what he wanted to say. It was like a jigsaw puzzle in which he was trying to force some of the pieces where they didn't fit.

Inspector Newman's bald announcement had irked him as much by the manner of its conveyance as by its content. On the other hand, he wished good luck to anyone who could successfully twist Shiv Kapur's tail. And who knows but his own murder enquiry might not benefit? Of course he would attend Newman's interrogation of Kapur; moreover, he had no intention of being a mere passive spectator, whatever D.I. Newman might expect.

He glanced at his watch. It was too late to call Rosa Epton at her office as she would have left for home by now.

He would phone her first thing in the morning to find out if she had received any word from young Arne.

When he did so, however, it was to be told that she would be out all day.

CHAPTER 35

Rosa walked resolutely up the short path to the front door and rang the bell. She was about to ring it a second time when she heard approaching footsteps within the house.

The door opened and a tall, austere-looking man faced her. He could only be Colonel Arne.

'I'm Rosa Epton,' she said. 'We've talked on the telephone.'

It was a long time since she had felt intimidated by anyone's appearance, but there was something particularly forbidding about the man who now stood staring at her as if she was an urchin who had impudently rung his doorbell.

'I'm your son's solicitor,' she added, when he didn't appear immediately to recognise her name.

He nodded briefly. 'I couldn't place you for a moment,' he said, in a voice as unwelcoming as his appearance.

As he continued to stand in the doorway, showing no sign of inviting her in, she said, 'Your son, Francis, wished me to come and see you.'

'Does that mean he's in trouble again?'

'He could be.' She paused. 'You did say when we spoke on the telephone, Colonel Arne, that you might be prepared to help him.'

'With his legal costs, you mean? My recollection is that you said the taxpayer was footing the bill.'

'You went on to say that you weren't the completely heartless person your son had probably made you out to be.'

'So you've come to put me to the test, is that it?'

'I've come at your son's request to have a talk with you,' Rosa said uncomfortably.

'Couldn't you have phoned in advance?'

'I could have, but decided not to.'

He gave her a suspicious look. 'I see. Well, I suppose you'd better come in.' Closing the front door behind her, he led the way into the drawing-room which looked out on to the garden at the rear of the house. 'And why did you decide to turn up unannounced? It's not like any solicitor in my experience to run the risk of a wasted journey.'

'Perhaps I'm an unusual sort of solicitor,' Rosa said in an embarrassed voice.

'So what is it my son has sent you to say to me?'

'When we spoke on the last occasion, you asked me if the police suspected Francis of Philip's murder and I told you that they had certainly questioned him about his movements that evening.'

'I remember that.'

'I believe he has now come under stronger suspicion.'

He looked across at her sharply. 'You mean they've discovered evidence which tells against him?'

'Previously they couldn't pin a motive on him, but they now have one – or think they have.'

'What is the motive?'

'That Francis killed his brother in the course of a furious quarrel over a drugs deal that went wrong.'

'You're telling me my sons were involved in drugs?'

'It would seem so.'

For several seconds he stared bleakly out of the window.

'I can't pretend to be surprised.'

'Not even about Philip's involvement?'

'I'm afraid Philip, too, lacked a sense of right and wrong. He was able to conceal it beneath a layer of charm which his younger brother never possessed, that's all.'

'I can't help noticing that you never refer to Francis by name,' Rosa observed.

'You notice correctly,' he said, and compressed his lips into a tight line as if to prevent the escape of any further words on the subject.

'What would your reaction be if Francis were to be charged with his brother's murder?' Rosa asked after an awkward silence.

He closed his eyes for a second as if the question had caused him a sudden stab of pain.

'I can't believe he did it,' he said gruffly.

'That won't stop the police charging him. They're looking for him at this moment in order to interrogate him further.'

'Looking for him, did you say?'

Rosa nodded. 'He's gone into temporary hiding.'

'But you've seen him and he asked you to come and see me?'

Rosa nodded again. 'Yes.'

'Why?'

'Because he believes that you, and only you, can help him.'

'In what way can I help him?' he asked tonelessly.

'I think you know the answer to that.'

He turned his head away and stared once more out of the window with an infinitely sad expression.

When he looked back at her, however, it was to say in a voice that was abruptly harsh, 'You must be more explicit.'

Rosa swallowed uncomfortably. She had undertaken her visit to Worthing with reluctance and trepidation. She had had no real idea of how she would be received, save that it was unlikely to be with either pleasure or warmth. She had even been prepared to have the front door shut in her face, though she reckoned (rightly, as it turned out) that his curiosity about her visit would get her into the house. Thereafter it was always going to be a sort of poker game between them, with Rosa hoping she held the stronger hand. There had been moments since her arrival, however, when she had been assailed by doubt. But now she was fully committed and there could be no turning back.

'Your son believes he knows who murdered his brother – and why.'

'That sounds a very bold statement. Perhaps you'd care to explain.'

Rosa licked her lips which had become dry. 'Francis went to see Philip on the evening he was murdered. They had a furious row about the drugs deal that had gone wrong, but Philip was still alive when Francis left. In fact he left because Philip more or less kicked him out, saying that he was expecting another visitor, but refusing to say who.' She paused. 'There seems little doubt that the person he was expecting turned out to be his murderer.' She gazed almost pleadingly at the man who was sitting and staring at her as if mesmerised by her words. 'Do I need to go on?' When he nodded, she added, 'I believe it was you Philip was expecting.'

'And supposing I say, rubbish?'

'Then Francis could be wrongfully charged with his brother's murder. Is that something which would lie comfortably on your conscience, Colonel Arne?'

'Aren't you being rather presumptuous in invoking my conscience?' He paused. 'You say it's my son's theory that I murdered Philip. Is it anything more than a theory?'

'Yes,' Rosa said quietly. 'He recently saw the Nicholas Hilliard miniature in a drawer in Shiv Kapur's flat. His inference is that Philip took it from here and gave it to Kapur to sell. He believes that, having discovered its loss, you visited Philip and demanded its return.'

'I see,' he said after an almost unbearable silence. 'So what are you proposing to do?'

'That depends on you, Colonel Arne.'

'The Nicholas Hilliard used to hang there,' he said, pointing at the wall to the left of the fireplace. 'I hung that other thing there to cover the patch. That fellow Sweet noticed it when he came here, but he never said anything and I suppose he didn't attach any particular importance to a patch on the wall. Because of its enormous value, sentimental as much as commercial – it was of an Elizabethan ancestor of my wife's – I put it away in a drawer after her death and then one day just after Philip had been here I found it missing. He had asked me where I'd put it and foolishly I told him, never dreaming that he would actually steal it. You said he *took* it, Miss Epton. You were wrong, he *stole* it, in order to sell it. I suppose he didn't think I'd miss it as soon as I did. Anyway, I phoned him and said I wanted a talk with him and he could probably guess what about. When I went to his flat that evening he was extremely truculent, said he'd already disposed of it and that his mother had always wished him to have it. He'd been fond of pointing out to visitors a likeness between himself and the ancestor in question, though I may say I never saw it myself. As I say, he was extremely truculent and aggressive and I'm afraid I saw red and seized the nearest thing to hand which was Lakshmi... Afterwards I drove back to Worthing and cleaned myself up. I had to destroy my trousers which were badly bloodstained. I should say that before leaving the flat I removed any fingerprints.' He stopped abruptly. 'That's about all.' He gave her a faintly quizzical look. 'So what are you going to do now?'

'Whatever you and your son may think of one another, he told me that you'd always been a man of honour and that you wouldn't let him be charged with a crime he didn't commit.'

'He said that, did he?' he remarked in a hollow voice. Then shaking his head slowly from side to side, he went on, 'It's almost as if there's been a curse on the male line of Arnes.' He shot Rosa a sudden glance. 'I suppose you think I'm no better than my two sons.'

'I'm not here to pass judgement, merely to try and ensure justice.'

'So what do you want me to do?'

'That has to be your decision. I can't dictate to you.'

'What you're really saying is I can either go to the police and confess to my son's murder or adopt another course which would amount to the same thing.'

Rosa was suddenly aware that she was shivering. She ached in every limb and didn't trust herself to speak. It was as if she were actively proffering him the means of self-destruction and the awareness of it struck her like a physical paralysis.

It seemed that each of them sat frozen in silent thought for several minutes. Then Colonel Arne got up stiffly and, without a word, walked to the door. Rosa followed him into the hall. There was nothing further to be said and her only desire was to get out of the house.

They shook hands like two strangers in a dream and a minute later she was back in her car. Colonel Arne had immediately closed the front door firmly behind her as if to symbolise his intentions.

Rosa found herself offering up a small incoherent prayer.

CHAPTER 36

Rosa went straight to court the next morning and didn't get into her office until around twelve-thirty.

'Detective Chief Inspector Sweet's been trying to reach you,' Stephanie said, as soon as Rosa made her return known. 'I told him where you were. Did he phone you at court?'

'No. I'd probably left before he called. I suppose you'd better get his number for me.'

'He said it was urgent. He didn't sound too pleased that you were out. I don't know whether he expects you to hang around in case he needs you.' Stephanie was given to such scornful comments on those whose manner affronted her.

Rosa felt nervous as she waited for Stephanie to obtain Sweet's number. For the past two nights Francis had stayed in the flat of a friend of hers who lived next door and who was away for three months. She had left Rosa her keys and told her to use her flat for visiting friends if she wished. Though Francis scarcely fell within that category, it seemed the best place to put him.

When she had returned from Worthing the previous evening she had found him lying on his stomach on the living-room floor watching television. A number of unwashed coffee cups were staked out around him.

'You can leave those, I'll do them,' he said with a touch of irritation when she immediately began to gather them up.

He followed her out into the kitchen where she gave him an account of her visit to his father.

For several seconds after she had finished he remained very still as he stared out of the window. Then, without a word, he had gone back into the living-room and resumed his posture in front of the television set.

Rosa made him some more coffee and took him a mug.

'I'll have to let Chief Inspector Sweet know tomorrow where you are. I'll arrange that we see him together,' she said, before taking her leave and going to her own flat next door.

But now that the moment had come to speak to Sweet, she found herself dreading the prospect. A dread occasioned in part by the fact that he had been trying to get in urgent touch with her and she could only guess at the reason.

'Detective Sergeant Adderly speaking,' a perky voice said when she was put through to Sweet's extension.

'It's Rosa Epton.'

'Ah,' Adderly said with a note of relief. 'Hold on, Miss Epton, Mr Sweet's just coming.'

Sweet's tone, by contrast, when he came on the line bore a note of frustration and hostility.

'I tried to reach you at court this morning,' he said accusingly, 'but they said you'd left. And you were out of your office all day yesterday. May I enquire where?'

Rosa frowned into the receiver.

'I'm not obliged to answer such a question, Mr Sweet, but if you're so anxious to know, I don't mind telling you. I was in Worthing.'

'Visiting Colonel Arne?'

'As a matter of fact, yes.'

'Have you been in touch with him since?'

'No.'

'Are you aware he's dead?'

There was a silence before Rosa said quietly, 'No, I didn't know that.'

'His housekeeper found his body when she arrived for work this morning. He had shot himself through the head with his old service revolver.'

179

'Did he leave a note?' Rosa asked in a tentative voice.

'Yes.'

'Then you know why he took his life?'

'That's precisely what I don't know. All the note said – and I quote – *Miss Rosa Epton, the London solicitor, can tell you what you want to know concerning my death.* Sweet paused before adding trenchantly, 'So now you know, Miss Epton, why I've been trying to get in touch with you urgently for most of the morning.'

When Sweet suggested that he and Adderly should come over to her office immediately, Rosa had readily agreed.

'We'll probably get to you quicker than you will to us,' he had said in a tone that seemed to imply that she might be tempted to play truant on the way.

They arrived about twenty minutes later. In the meantime she had sent out for sandwiches and coffee to ease what seemed likely to be an awkward interview.

It took her about a quarter of an hour to give an account of her visit to Colonel Arne. When she finished, Sweet was thoughtful for a while.

'I'm bound to say,' he remarked at last, 'that it's a great pity you didn't bring the information to us rather than go rushing off like some private eye in a bad T.V. serial. If you had done so, Colonel Arne might still be alive.'

'In the first place it wasn't so much information as supposition and I had to test it for myself. And, secondly, I did nothing to dissuade Colonel Arne from going to the police station and making a confession, if that was what he wished to do.'

'You're not telling me you seriously expected him to do that, are you?'

'No. But the choice of action was always his.' She paused and went on with a note of sadness, 'I don't imagine he could face spending the rest of his days in prison. And it certainly wasn't a fate I would have wished on him.' She gave Sweet a small, quizzical smile. 'My guess is that you feel the same way, Mr Sweet.'

'Perhaps I do,' he said with a faint shrug 'Incidentally, while you were busy at Worthing, we weren't exactly idle. Shiv Kapur has been charged with various offences in connection with false passports and visas, the sale of which was obviously his main activity behind the façade of the Reynolds-Bailey Trust. It seems fairly clear that Philip Arne was involved to some extent as well. I suspect that Mister Kapur will seek to throw most of the blame on him seeing that he's not around to deny it.'

'I take it there's no evidence that Francis Arne was also involved?'

'I would say, Miss Epton,' Sweet remarked dryly, 'that your client is one of the most fortunate young men who has crossed swords with the police for some time.'

'I've already told him that and I shall tell him again. I shall also advise him against making any formal complaint against those two officers in his case. My final advice to him will be to get away from London.'

'I hope he'll listen to you. But what I was going on to tell you was that when we searched Kapur's flat we found the miniature you've referred to. Of course, most of us being only simple coppers we had no idea of its value.'

'I was pretty sure it was a Nicholas Hilliard,' Adderly broke in. He had been showing increasing signs of restiveness and Sweet's provocative observation detonated his bottled-up eagerness to display his knowledge.

'What about his girl-friend?' Rosa asked.

'Nadia? She'll probably be needed as a witness. She's obviously under Kapur's domination, but I'm sure she can be persuaded where her best interests lie,' Sweet said with a cynical grin. He leaned forward and took another sandwich. 'I'll still need a statement from young Arne and one from you, too, Miss Epton. I imagine, however, you'd like to write your own concerning your visit to Worthing yesterday.'

Rosa nodded. 'I'll do that this afternoon and let you have it.'

'You realise you'll have to attend the inquest in due course.' He got up and patted his stomach. 'All those sandwiches and here I am, trying to lose weight! But thank you all the same, Miss Epton.' He moved toward the door. 'It's funny, you know, but when I called on Colonel Arne I noticed a bare patch on the wall where some small object had recently hung. More importantly I became aware of Colonel Arne intercepting my gaze and deliberately moving so as to hide it from my line of vision. I thought about it afterwards, but that was as far as I got.' He sighed. 'There's a lesson there for young detective sergeants like Paul Adderly.' Sergeant Adderly smiled dutifully and Sweet went on, 'Except, of course, he'd have realised at once that it was a Nicholas Hilliard which had been removed from the wall. You're a walking encyclopedia of useless knowledge, aren't you, Paul?'

Rosa gave Adderly a sympathetic wink. It seemed to her that Sweet was being unnecessarily cruel to his sergeant. Adderly's return wink, however, went further than required to assure her. Perhaps Sweet knew best after all, she reflected.

It was about two months later she received a postcard from Devon. It read:

Perry and I are living on a commune. Both it and he are driving me mad. If I stay much longer, you'll have me back as a client. Francis.

The picture on the face of the card was of an idyllically peaceful stretch of water. Francis had drawn in the figure of a girl, obviously meant to be herself, sitting on the ground gazing across the water. Behind her, ready to pounce, he had drawn a small leering satyr with a malevolent grin which was clearly meant to represent himself.

As she studied the picture with wry amusement, she felt it was probably the first time he had actually succeeded in communicating with her.

>>> If you've enjoyed this book and would like to discover more great vintage crime and thriller titles, as well as the most exciting crime and thriller authors writing today, visit: >>>

The Murder Room
Where Criminal Minds Meet

themurderroom.com

www.ingramcontent.com/pod-product-compliance
Ingram Content Group UK Ltd.
Pitfield, Milton Keynes, MK11 3LW, UK
UKHW040436280225
455666UK00003B/103